AN APOLOGY TO
LUCIFER

Wayne E Haley
Sean P Haley

B. X. VARĐS

Published by:
D. X. Varos, Ltd
7665 E. Eastman Ave. #B101
Denver, CO 80231

Book cover design and layout by D. X. Varos
using images ©Shutterstock:
Red Quill Image #1276414330
Tipped Inkwell #43090702
Ink Stain #649919185

ISBN: 978-1-955065-19-1 (paperback)
ISBN: 978-1-955065-20-7 (ebook)

To endless nights dancing with madness, I owe so much which I can never repay to my beloved Kathleen, Alicia, and Gwen – Wayne

To my consummate cheerleaders and sounding boards: Kristy, Doreen, and Gracie - Sean

Prologue

The sky exploded as electric blue flashes cleaved through the cosmos. From the edge of the universe, the Ancient Ones, roaring screams of delight, looked on and hoped for their moment. A breach in the Crystal Sphere was all they needed to return and finish what they had started long ago.

The last of the angels stood tightly together, each covered with wounds that were smeared with their own and others' blood, for they had seen their brothers fall and perish at the barrier, never to return.

A thousand turns of the celestial clock had not reined in the destruction that had started as an argument and was being finished as an act of genocide.

Under the red banner with a black dragon stood the last rampart. Weary of the loathsome slaughter, angels cleaned their swords and tightened the straps on their breastplates, waiting for their next engagement. Across the scene of fallen bodies and broken stones walked one with purpose and determination. His purple cloak hung around his imposing frame, and his curly blond hair fell over his shoulders. Lucifer's piercing blue eyes surveyed what was left of his once-great cohort. Blood dripped from his hands, and he wiped them on his robe.

He approached a single angel, Astaroth, who was down on one knee holding his sword with both hands and watching the moving clouds that concealed his enemy. Lucifer stood behind him and said quietly, "You confronted Michael. Did you consign him to the depths?"

"No, my Lord. A deep cut in the chest... but it was not enough." The kneeling Astaroth turned his face to look upon Lucifer. "We are finished here. I would suggest, my Lord, you take the terms offered and save yourself and the others that remain."

"The *terms*." Lucifer turned and looked upon his comrades and then back to Astaroth. "What of you? You do not want to be part of what I can save?"

"I will choose a different road back to this place... if my Lord permits it." Astaroth ran his bloodied hand through his long brown hair.

"Even the worst of terms here would have to be better than the terms you would choose, my brother." Lucifer reached out and placed his hand on Astaroth's shoulder.

Astaroth sheathed his sword and rose, turning to look at his companions.

"Time is moving about us, my Lord. I shall have to accept the will of the universe before I would stand and see you disgraced. But you must survive all of this; for certain, our time shall come again. And it appears *He* is unwilling to accept that something far more destructive than this quarrel lies in wait."

Lucifer turned and spoke to the others. "Those who choose to go with Astaroth, go now, for we shall not be here very long." The clouds were parting, and the enemy, led by a wounded Michael, appeared before them.

"Until then...that I may find you again, my Lord." The two embraced one last time. Astaroth plummeted from the height over the edge of the abyss. His final words as an angel, an apology to Lucifer for failing him, and an eternal pledge for redemption.

Chapter 1

At the stroke of midnight, the Apostolic Library of the Vatican was completely empty, except for a single guard that roamed among four buildings. The darkness was only offset by the sporadic glow of the emergency exit lights that hung above doorways, reflecting off the marble floors. The same floors had been purposefully designed to intensify the grandiose echoes of the steel-soled footfalls of the crusaders who had traveled these halls for nearly a thousand years.

In between alcoves of the room, the two men met where they would remain unseen and their whispering voices unheard. As they approached one another, one of the men bowed to the other in respect, though both were cardinals of the Church of Rome.

"Please tell me it is true, brother," Cardinal Anton Baptist Zimmerman said as he shook his counterpart's hand.

The younger man, Cardinal Francis Santorini spoke in low and furtive tones. "It is. We have finally located it."

Zimmerman's eyes lit up with a strange mixture of emotion. "After all this time, the tides are about to turn." His eyes drifted past Santorini and fixated on the painting behind him. "Where is the book?"

"It is apparently in the custody of one of our own." Cardinal Santorini revealed a slight smile. "A Father Albert Kennedy, at All Saints College in Boston."

Zimmerman looked at Santorini, almost in disbelief at their good fortune. "Can we send *her* to retrieve it?"

"We are working on getting in touch with her now. Evidently, she is currently on assignment by her *other* employer." Santorini's words carried a noticeable element of disdain. "In Venice."

Cardinal Zimmerman took the other man by the shoulder, looking into his eyes with a determined gaze. "My brother," he said forcefully, making sure there was no room for ambiguity in what he would say next. "There is nothing on this earth more important than collecting that book. Send word to her we will increase our usual payment two-fold, and make sure she knows it's urgent." The cardinal took a deep breath before continuing in an even tone: "I ask you now to go and make very sure this takes place."

As the two men parted ways, Zimmerman walked up to the painting he had been staring at, *The Abyss of Hell*. It was Botticelli's illustration of Hell to accompany Dante's *Inferno*. Dante's Hell was an abyss, a giant cave leading to the center of the Earth, that God created when he cast Lucifer out of Heaven. In the illustration, Lucifer is stuck in the center, caught in ice. Zimmerman stared at it for a few moments, then thought to himself, *You almost had it right.*

Chapter 2

Father Thomas Morelli was sitting quietly in St. Mark's Square in Venice at a small open-air café, sipping a glass of wine and scribbling down notes in a book. Spring was about to give way to summer, but the height of tourist season had not yet descended on the ancient, sinking city. Still, crowds of visitors with cell phones, cameras, and every kind of recording device imaginable, were walking past Thomas's table, hurrying to the next sight they had to see before moving on to another point of interest.

Thomas's trip to Venice was entirely different than that of these tourists. His purpose was purely research, an investigation into the life of Giordano

Bruno, the Renaissance mystic who was burned alive as a heretic in Rome's Campo de' Fiori during the Inquisition. Bruno was a provocative subject for historians, undoubtedly from a Catholic perspective. Bruno believed the universe was infinite and populated by many worlds. He thought the sun was just one of an endless number of independently moving heavenly bodies, and he was the first man to state stars seen at night were identical to the Sun. Bruno also agreed with Copernicus that the Earth moved. He was outspoken about his beliefs in reincarnation and thought philosophy was the discipline of the elite, and religion was the instruction for the ignorant, all of which placed him in a continual state of sin against God and the crosshairs of the Holy Office.

Bruno was a magnificent example of someone caught between two worlds who succumbed to the imprudence of believing he would be protected because he offered up truth. Thomas had spent five years researching and reading everything he could to complete his book on Bruno. It was nothing short of a demand for the Church to reconsider the verdict and judgment it had imposed upon Bruno and openly recant the error, as they did in the case of Galileo. Thomas knew all too well this book would be taken as an assault on the Holy See of Rome, and his being a member of the clergy only made it worse.

It was only during this trip to Venice that Thomas discovered, hidden away in the repository of a church, key documents spelling out the way Bruno had been betrayed and wrongly portrayed to the Vatican. Worse yet, his betrayer was someone close to him, who, in exchange for Bruno's "demonic" journal, had been granted immunity by the Holy Office. This fact had been the missing piece of Thomas' book.

The subsequent interviews and denunciations that followed had all played out in this majestic place, just across the square from where Thomas now sat. *A lot has changed since then,* Thomas thought, looking up over the square. As he surveyed his surroundings, Thomas caught his reflection in the café window. His crystal blue eyes stared back at him. Dark stubble covered his chiseled jaw. Around his temples, patches of gray was making its way deeper into the brush of thick brown hair. At six feet tall and one hundred and ninety pounds, Thomas was in reasonably good shape. He mused, *Not bad for an old boxer, even if you are turning fifty this year.* Thomas grinned and re-immersed himself into his notes, failing to notice the tall, tanned brunette in the sleek black dress and Louboutin heels who had approached his table and was staring down at his writings. That is, until she moved slightly, and her shadow drifted across his table.

As Thomas looked up, a shudder passed through him. She was breathtaking. Her raven-black hair hung below her shoulders, and her face was radiant. Red lipstick contrasted with her olive complexion, while intense dark lashes accentuated her brown eyes. She smiled at Thomas. "May I join you, Father, for just a moment? I won't take much of your time. Just a brief conversation is all I ask."

"Please." Thomas stood up, gesturing toward the chair across from him.

"Thank you. I am Lorenza Pellegrini, and I believe you are the priest who is writing the book about Master Bruno?"

Thomas motioned to the waiter, who briskly worked his way over to where they were sitting. Thomas ordered a glass of wine for her, and she nodded in agreement that his choice was acceptable.

"I am Father—"

She held up her hand to stop him and waited until the waiter had returned, which seemed like only moments later. He placed the glass of wine and another glass of water on the table making it clear he was at her service if she needed anything else. She smiled and dismissed him with grace that takes years to cultivate, and yet she did not appear to be over twenty-five. "I know who you are, Father, and that is why I am here." She sipped her wine and then placed a pair of designer sunglasses upon her face.

"If you know that, then you have a decided advantage. Why would you be interested in speaking with a time-worn researcher like me?" Thomas sat back and waited, hoping this was not a come-on for buying a timeshare; worse yet, she might be looking for a confessor in the middle of St. Mark's Square.

"My Master would like to speak with you," she stated casually. She looked around the café and then picked up her wine glass, only to hold it in mid-air.

She turned and stared directly into Thomas's eyes after pulling her sunglasses down slightly so that their eyes made contact. "I think you would find the appointment extremely interesting."

"Quite an unusual word choice, don't you think? Referring to someone as your 'Master.'" Thomas felt a slight degree of uneasiness creep over him.

"But that is what he is. No other description would do. However that is beside the point. He requests you accompany me to his villa, just off the Grand Canal, and there, he will explain why he desires so much to speak with you." She pushed her sunglasses back up her nose to cover her eyes once again. As she turned her head, Thomas looked upon her profile and noted the well-formed physique that went with it.

"There seems to be a mistake. I am sure I am not the person whom you are trying to obtain for your *employer*." Thomas said, trying to change the context for his own sake more than anything else.

"He told me to inform you that if you do come, he will permit you to inspect his private library. The three unpublished, original manuscripts Master Bruno composed while he was here in Venice and the correspondence between Master Bruno and Dr. Dee. He emphasizes that he has never let anyone else see these artifacts." She paused for a fraction of a moment. "I don't believe the offer will be extended again if you decline, and that would be a shame, to say the least."

"The Inquisition burned those books. No one has ever been known to have a copy of the three books you mention." Thomas felt an edge of irritation begin to build within him. He did not want to be played as a fool by anyone, no matter how beautiful they may be.

"Then I am to tell my Master you are not interested in seeing them or meeting with him." She stood up and extended her hand. "It truly is a pity. For he knows more about Master Bruno than all the people you have dealt with up to now, and I shall suffer his anger at your rejection."

Thomas stood up and took her hand, holding it longer than mere politeness dictates. "What do you mean you will suffer his anger?"

"My Master does not tolerate failure on the part of his attendants...no matter how much he cares for them." She turned to leave as another chill passed through him. Thomas could not in good conscience let this young woman be fired from her position because he was calcified in his belief the books she referred to did not exist.

"Where? Where do I have to go to meet with your...?" Thomas paused as he searched for the right word. Unwilling to use "Master," he stuttered.

"With me." She motioned to a boat tied up by the square. Its driver sat smoking on the bow, apparently waiting.

"All right." Thomas picked up his notes and stuffed them into his briefcase, which had been sitting on the adjoining table. "I will go with you and see what this is all about." As he reached into his pocket for a couple of euros for the wine, he heard the waiter speak behind him.

"No, Father. I have taken care of it. Please have a nice day with your beautiful companion." The waiter was already clearing the glasses and smiling at Thomas.

"Thank you very much, but here –" Thomas extended a bill to him for a tip, but the man, still smiling, simply walked away. Thomas tucked the briefcase up under his arm and started walking to where the woman was waiting. When he caught up to her, she wrapped her arm through his and continued walking toward the boat. Embarrassed, Thomas felt the back of his neck redden but made no attempt to remove her arm.

As they walked, Lorenza spoke about statues, buildings, shops, and fountains Thomas had never noticed before. They stepped into the sleek, mahogany runabout, and she sat in the back, crossing her legs as Thomas sat beside her. Lorenza pointed to the islands off the coast and told him captivating tales about the monks who once occupied the monastery. She re-looped her arm through his as they slowly worked their way up the Grand Canal toward the Rialto Bridge before turning up a small side canal. Slowly, the boat moved through a watery avenue of stone buildings, so close on both sides Thomas could have reached out and touched them. This ancient waterway was rich with history. The canal they headed up was not one of the main canals, but rather, a small one used by individuals with boat docks under their homes. As the driver eased the elegant craft into a stall below a three-story villa, Thomas watched the painting on the wall at the landing stage come alive. The wall fresco depicted a party held in a grand court. The paint was faded, but the details were still visible on the plaster.

"Someone told me Raphael painted that so he would not starve to death while he was here. I don't know if the story is true, but the painting is lovely," Lorenza said as she stepped from the boat with ease. She took Thomas's hand and helped him navigate the step up from the boat.

"Is this a museum?" Thomas asked once he was on the solid footing of the stone walkway.

She laughed and looked around. "It could be. But no, it is the house of my Master. His family has owned it since before the Great Expansion in Venice. It is filled with relics museums worldwide would pay greatly for, but he is too sentimental to sell them. They remind him of generations gone by." She moved up a flight of stairs to an ornate, dark-colored door that opened very quietly despite its heft onto a marble-floored entryway and a large room lit only by candles. Thomas followed her, holding his briefcase under his arm.

This is like going back to the sixteenth century, Thomas thought as he stepped inside. All the furnishings, wall hangings, and carpets were magnificent. The carpet alone should have been under glass on a wall instead of being walked on. It was hand-woven and knotted in Persia by someone who had been dead for at least four centuries. Thomas thought the ceiling paintings were a match for anything done in Florence or Rome. The subtle scent of a rare incense drifted through the air.

"Come, Padre, I have something to show you." Lorenza dropped her bag in a chair and walked into another room; she opened the wooden shutters and light and a warm breeze filled the room, which Thomas saw overlooked the Grand Canal. Thomas was standing in a library with perhaps ten thousand volumes of old, leather-bound books. Glancing down the aisles, he saw masterpieces of literature he had only read about in catalogs, works whose facsimiles appeared in libraries around the world. Some of the volumes were supposedly lost, destroyed in fires or at the hands of madmen. Thomas wondered why these were exposed to the elements. *These should be in a temperature-controlled environment*, Thomas thought. "My God! What a collection! These are priceless!" Thomas turned in a slow circle, taking in the scope of the room with unabashed awe.

"Yes. Many were published here in Venice from originals brought from far away, smuggled by traders who sold them for as much gold as rare spices and jade would bring. The printers here were renowned for their ability to copy them exactly. All of this occurred despite the watchful eyes of the Church, which was constantly trying to seek out and rid the world of controversial texts. Many a tormented soul perished because of their work on such material. But what I want to show you is on the desk, here." She pulled a brown leather chair out from behind the sizable desk and motioned for him to sit down in it.

Thomas quietly examined the desk, which appeared to be hand-carved from some African hardwood. In the center of it were four manuscripts, all bound in leather with gold-edged paper. He dropped his briefcase onto the floor next to his feet and sank into the chair. Leaning forward, he opened the first book and read the title leaf. It was handwritten. Smiling, he proceeded to look at the next one. It, too, was handwritten. Cynicism swelled within him. He obliged it by looking at the remaining two volumes and then closed them as he sat back smiling. *The perfect setting for this trick,* he thought.

"Well? What do you think?" Lorenza's eyes sparkled and danced.

"My dear, I think you are wonderful and this place is the ideal setting. But both you and I know you should not try to play this kind of trick on someone who has spent a lifetime in study. A collector would probably begin pulling out his checkbook and offering a king's ransom for these books. But I have spent too long combing through libraries and dusty old basements to be drawn into a game like this. Besides, I am but a poor researcher who could not pay for the cost of the reproduction, let alone a copy itself." Thomas leaned forward and looked at her face.

"I don't understand. You are not happy to see these, nor do you want to read them?" Lorenza looked questioningly at him. "My Master thought you would be delighted to see the originals of these texts."

"These books could not exist. This copy here, for instance..." Thomas pulled the second one out and opened it. "It was printed here in Venice. There were twenty-one copies made before the deranged monks of the Inquisition found it being printed and arrested the printer. They then burned all the copies along with the original. It is referenced in other sources, but no one has ever seen the original. So, this may be a wonderful copy of something, but it is not Bruno's. He even lamented its destruction."

"There were twenty-two printed, and the Inquisition did not destroy the original, but rather a copy of the original. *That* is the original –" she pointed to the book on the desk – "written by Bruno himself. And this..." She moved to the library wall, pulled a large black edition from the shelf, and placed it on the desk in front of him. "This is the twenty-second one. Printed by Brunewli. Please..." She motioned for Thomas to open it. As he did, his jaw dropped almost imperceptibly.

Thomas had been consulted several times by collectors and libraries to authenticate manuscripts printed in Venice. He opened the flyleaf to see the printer's seal. He looked carefully at the paper and then moved onto the text itself. He was way out of his depth here. *This had to be the greatest forgery anyone has ever done,* he thought. The paper was perfect, the typeface exact, and when he looked at the page from an angle, he noticed the watermark only Brunewli used.

While Thomas studied the paper through a magnifying glass Lorenza had offered him, she pulled three additional books from the shelves and set them down on the desk. They were printed editions of the three handwritten manuscripts on the desk he had initially looked at with skepticism. Thomas compared the handwritten copies with the printed ones and found they matched exactly.

An older woman as beautiful as Lorenza entered the room. Her silver-gray hair was immaculate, and her perfectly tailored light pastel suit hugged her trim body. She placed a tea service and some small pastries on a sideboard in the room. She nodded to Lorenza, who smiled at her in thanks, then she walked from the room with the same elegance Lorenza had displayed.

"Tea?" Lorenza offered and waited.

"Please. No cream, only lemon." Thomas stood up and walked to the window. His head was swimming. *Could it be? Could these volumes have escaped the fires of prejudice and survived all those years hidden here?* Thomas felt Lorenza next to him and turned to face her. She was holding a cup of tea for him and looking at his profile.

"You seem to think this is some kind of a game; that someone wants to take something from you, when in reality, it is just the opposite. Someone wishes to give you something. But the world we live in does not accept favors as the norm anymore, does it?" Lorenza turned and started to leave the room. She stopped to glance back at Thomas. "Look at them; read them. They are here for you to examine, that is all. If you find them important to your work, then I have accomplished my task, and I am better off for it. Maria will get you anything you need, and when you are ready to return to your hotel, Carlos will take you there. If you so desire, you may stay here tonight, and we will make a room available for you. After you start reading, Carlos will go to your hotel and gather your belongings if you find you need more time. You are welcome here for as long or as short of a time as you desire." She turned and, without another word, left through the double doors at the end of the room.

Thomas stood there looking out into the Grand Canal. *What rabbit hole did I just fall into?*

Chapter 3

Thomas sat at the desk quietly, reading the calligraphic script on the pages of the first book. The phrasing was remarkably correct. The word usage was entirely within the exact timeframe, and the accent marks duplicated Bruno's down to the smallest dot. Thomas was still skeptical, but as the words flowed across each page, they sounded...no, they *felt* as if Bruno was speaking them. *If this was a forgery, then the person who did it had an insight into Bruno's mind no one has ever seen.* On the margins of the text were comments in the same handwriting in Italian, French, and German. These notes indicated changes he wished to make to a particular paragraph or sentence, and as Thomas checked the printed volume, he was amazed to find the changes had been made. *This had to be his first draft—the one he used to prepare the second copy and the one found at the printers.* The implication of this startling fact was beyond anything Thomas could imagine. These texts would become the basis for his book, and if he could use them or make copies of them to prove their existence, *My work would have substantiation without comparison!* Thomas froze. *I dare not have such heady thoughts.* Pride is a sin, and within a priest of the Church of Rome, it can either mark one for isolation in a small African village or the red robes of a cardinal.

The afternoon wore on with Thomas' briefcase open and notebooks littering the desk next to the priceless works. Occasionally, Thomas sat back and watched the boats going by on the liquid road bisecting the city. The evening was approaching, and the larger groups of tourists had ebbed to the stream of workers who were now leaving the city. As Thomas stood at the window, the door opened, and Maria came in, holding a candle lighter in her hand. She began to light several large candles around the room, and as she did so, she closed many of the windows and shutters. Then, she walked up to the desk and lit the seven large candles upon it.

"It will make it easier for you to read. Would Father like to have something to eat in here, or should I have a place in the dining room set for you?" She smiled at Thomas.

24

Thomas took his gold watch from his pocket and realized it was nearly eight-thirty. He had spent well over seven hours within this room and suddenly felt a twinge of embarrassment overcome him. He looked at his notes beside the open manuscript on the desk, not sure how to answer the question.

"I did not realize how late it was. I have overstayed my welcome, I am sure. It is just so fantastic; it is hard to break away." His words came from the heart, and he honestly did not know what to do. If he left now, would he ever be able to come back and see these books again? "I was supposed to meet the owner of this house today as well, and I did not notice the time."

"The Master was delayed elsewhere but notified us to make every accommodation for you so you could fully enjoy yourself with the books. There is no problem with dinner or with you staying here. Truly." She smiled again and added: "I had Carlos pick up your things at the hotel and bring them here. I have a very nice room on the third floor with a view of the city and the canal. It is very comfortable, and we can provide you with all you need."

Evidently, these people handle things in a completely different way than most. "Oh, that was very considerate of you. But I need to go back to my hotel and settle up the account there."

"Oh, Father, that has been done. It was the least the Master could do since he could not be here to meet with you. Consider yourself at home here. Work as late as you want, and when you are ready,

25

one of us will show you to your room. Carlos has laid out your things and added some extra items of clothing that will make working here a little easier. The Master was sure it would take you at least three or four days to go through the texts and find the supporting references in the library here." She smiled again and looked almost childlike in her enjoyment of the situation and her role in it. "Now about dinner...here or in the dining room?"

"Something simple would be fine. Some bread and cheese would do." Thomas felt he had imposed on his host too much already.

"Nonsense. The cook has prepared a lovely duck with wild rice, and Carlos went downstairs to find a bottle of claret. If you would like to wash up, there is a facility just outside those doors to the right. Dinner should be ready about thirty minutes from now. I will call for you when it is time." She picked up the tray of tea and left without another word. Thomas stood there feeling very strange. Maria was timeless; her beauty was deep and warm, aloof yet approachable.

Thomas sat back down at the desk and continued to work by candlelight. The text pulled him in. He found Bruno's words thrilling and delightful, even with his degree of arrogance. A few minutes later, Carlos came in holding a heavy scholar's robe and offered it to Thomas, to ward off the chill in the air. He lit a fire in the fireplace and made sure it was burning well, before leaving without a word. Thomas pulled the robe on and found it fit like a well-worn sweater. He tied the sash around his waist and continued reading by candlelight, catching the occasional murmur of a boat passing in the night.

Thomas had stopped taking notes, reasoning that since he had committed himself to stay here, he could work through all of the text first and then go back later and make the notes necessary to complete his own text. He had surrendered to this old, grand house and the invitation from a perfect stranger who had made him feel so comfortable so quickly.

It had been a long time since Thomas had truly enjoyed himself in this way. The words flowed across the pages, and he felt as though he was sitting next to Master Bruno as he was writing the truths he wished for the world to understand. Thomas touched one of the pages and ran his hand down it, realizing Bruno's hand had rested on this very page as his quill pen wrote the words Thomas now read. *It was no wonder the Church had feared this man so much. His vision of the universe was that of a free thinker.* Thomas found himself sinking deeper into the chair and reading the Latin with fluency. Bruno's was a way of writing that made one unable to stop turning pages one after another.

"Father..." Maria said as she stood across the desk from Thomas, trying hopelessly to get his attention. "Father, it is time for dinner."

Thomas pulled his head up from the book that had captured him. He looked at her for a moment without recognition. Then, the present came back to him. "I am sorry. I was so..." He struggled for the right word.

"Engrossed? Would that do?" She smiled and motioned for him to follow her. He did so without further comment. Thomas did not know what to speak to her about, so they walked in silence. After a moment, she broke it by saying: "There is a wonderful little group playing Brahms across the Grand Canal, so you should have some entertainment with dinner tonight."

"That is wonderful." Thomas followed her down a candlelit hallway into a formal dining room with a table nearly twenty feet long. There was one place setting on it by the window where the music filtered in. Thomas stood there for a moment, looking around. "You are not joining me, Maria?"

"Oh no, Father. It would not be right. I will have your dinner served right away. Thank you." And with that, she was gone.

Thomas sat down and looked at the bottle of wine next to his plate. It was a local vintage from 1968: *a rare find—a fifty-year-old bottle of wine for a simple dinner for one.* It seemed a shame, but it was already uncorked, so Thomas poured a glassful and tasted its delicate nature and body.

As Thomas sipped the wine, he wondered, *Just who exactly is this mystery man, my host?* It seemed he had stepped out of modernity and into another time and place: a house with no electricity lit by candles; music playing from an unseen group which easily could have been behind the choir screen in any significant church in the world; a bottle of wine worth more than he made in a year. Thomas had obtained a grant to do this research, and the money was intended to be used for travel, lodging, and food while he was gone. Any day like today when he received generosity - like a roof over his head and a meal - meant an additional day he could fund his quest to its end. For a moment, Thomas almost felt guilty about accepting all of this, but how it was presented to him left him with a feeling there was a higher hand at work. Just as the thought occurred, it was gone, as the wine slowly began to have its effect. Thomas relaxed in his chair, listening to the music across the canal.

A waiter introduced himself as 'Mario' as he came into the room dressed in a short white dinner jacket and black tie. He told Thomas he would be serving him tonight. Thomas started to stand, and Mario gently pushed him back down into his chair. "I am here to serve you, Father. Please." He rolled a cart into the dining room and placed in front of Thomas an array of dishes, including a salad, a plate of duck with wild rice, and asparagus with a cream sauce. Then, he put down a loaf of warm bread and a small bowl of whipped butter next to it. He also placed a bell on the table. "If there is anything you desire, please ring this, and I will come immediately." He bowed and was gone.

Thomas started slowly. When the first bite of duck hit his palate, he was entirely seduced by the skill of the chef who had prepared this meal. Each bite was like a carnival of tastes parading inside his mouth. By the time he finished his meal and the bottle of wine, Thomas felt as if he had just committed some sin, but he told himself it was all right. He felt a little unbalanced from the wine but not out of control. A few moments later, Thomas realized he had finished the bottle by himself.

Thomas had started to walk back to the library when Carlos stopped him in the foyer. He was standing there as if he had been waiting for Thomas to arrive. "Excuse me, Father, for interrupting you, but I thought it a good time to show you to your room. It is up these stairs...if you would follow me, please." Carlos immediately started up the circular stairway, and Thomas followed him up to the third floor very quickly. "Your room is here."

Carlos opened the door and gestured for Thomas to enter. It was a suite rather than a room. It contained a four-poster bed with a canopy and several chairs of various designs, all appearing sturdy and well suited for comfort. A small sideboard with his grooming items was already laid out for him, and a large armoire stood open, displaying not only his clothing, but several other new garments. Thomas noticed several new dark gray silk shirts and various sweaters matching the new black slacks.

"Dr. Pellegrini had me pick those up for your comfort. A gift, Father. She thought that while you were here, you should be comfortable and not committed to wearing your Roman collars." Carlos smiled and handed Thomas a key for the door. "If you wish to lock it...if not, the maid will clean it up for you each morning." Carlos turned and held up his hand to halt Thomas. "One more thing, please. An indulgence is needed from you for just a moment. If you would be so good as to close your eyes and not make any sudden moves. You will feel something in your hand. This is very important. Please hold out your hand."

Thomas closed his eyes and held out his hand. So far, Thomas had only found grace and hospitality within these walls and saw no reason to fear Carlos for his request. A strange roughness ran down the back of his hand twice. It was moist and felt almost like very light sandpaper.

"Thank you. You may open your eyes now...but please don't jump." Carlos stood there, close to Thomas. At his side was a leopard with its beautiful green eyes looking up into his face and rubbing its tongue around its mouth. "This is Aza. He works as our security system for the house. At night we let him out to roam at will. If you don't want him in your room, then lock the door. If you just close it, he can get up and open the door. Once he has tasted you as he just did, he will never forget the taste. You can come and go from this house at will now, and he will never bother you. At worst, he will be a nuisance in wanting to be rubbed all the time."

"Wasn't Aza a fallen angel who taught men magic?" Thomas asked while rubbing the cat's head; he started to purr.

31

"I don't know about such things, Father. I am sorry. I am good at the things I do, but I don't claim scholarship among them. You should ask Dr. Pellegrini when she returns from her trip to the United States. She named him for us." Carlos patted the massive cat on his side. "Aza, leave the good Father in peace, now." The cat got up and walked from the room. It turned and made eye contact with Thomas again, before strolling off down the hallway.

"Interesting security system. So, Lorenza has a doctorate? In what—do you know?" Thomas asked, now looking very relaxed.

"Medieval literature. Dr. Pellegrini graduated at the top of her class at the University of Milan. She reads, writes, and speaks at least four languages along with Latin and Greek. Like you, Dr. Pellegrini can take one of those old books and read it like a novel. Besides being one of the most beautiful women in Venice, she is probably one of the smartest. Like you, Dr. Pellegrini came here to study the old books, and she has never left. The Master offered her a position, and she took it. That has been maybe ten years now." Carlos turned to leave and motioned for Thomas to pass him first.

"How can that be? She cannot be older than twenty-five or twenty-six years of age."

"Oh no, Father. Last year we celebrated her thirty-fifth birthday. People from all over Europe came here for it. I worked throughout the night, shuttling people back and forth from all over Venice for the party. She takes good care of herself and stays fit."

"By the way, Carlos, what do I owe you for cleaning up my room and paying my bill at the hotel?" Thomas spoke to the man's back as he walked down the stairs.

"Nothing, Father. Once they knew you were staying here, the hotel waived your room fees...even for the nights you had already stayed there. They put the refund right back onto your Visa card." At the foyer, Carlos started to leave through the side door where Thomas had initially entered.

"Well, I must owe you something. And why would the hotel do that?" Thomas inquired.

"Since the Master owns the hotel where you were staying, it only seemed correct. And before you ask me about the new clothing in the room...the items came from my cousin's tailor shop. He would not even have the shop if it weren't for the Master. So please, no more talk of money. You are an honored guest here, which means we will get you anything you desire without you ever reaching into your pocket. That is the Master's way of doing things. If you need anything tonight, just pull the cord behind the desk, and I will come. If there is nothing you need now, I shall say good night." Carlos touched his forehead with a finger and left quietly.

Thomas walked back into the library and saw Aza lying by the desk. He walked around to the other side to sit down. Aza rolled his head over and looked up at him. He yawned and lay back down on the carpet. As Thomas looked around the candlelit room, with the wild cat sleeping peacefully on the floor, he could imagine this same scene reoccurring in any of the past six centuries in this house. It was a surrealistic moment; however, two thoughts kept circling in his mind: *Who exactly is this Master? And why am I here?*

Chapter 4

The next two days passed rather quickly for Thomas as he immersed himself in the texts. He ate, slept, and worked without interruption. The only time he left the villa was to charge his phone and laptop at the café down the canal. It had crossed his mind he would not be able to take the books out of the villa and show them to the world. Therefore, he needed his phone charged for photographing face plates and critical pages of the books and getting shots of them from various angles to prove their existence.

He was rapidly filling his notebook, and he could not believe how quickly his own book was coming together now. Thomas found no heresy within the pages; they were the work of a glorious mind—a man who understood more than anyone else of his time. As Thomas continued reading the texts, the question radiated in his mind with increasing urgency. *Why? Why did the Church kill you? You recanted, just as Galileo did, yet you suffered a much different fate.* If the strategy behind his soon-to-be-completed book was implemented correctly, Thomas figured like Galileo, the Church would have to make an open statement about the quality of Bruno's work and their misjudgment—or at least admit the improper handling of the case. In his heart, Thomas believed the Church had unfairly murdered Bruno, and it was time to clear his record.

Earlier that day, he had received a message from Lorenza asking him to stay a few more days until she returned from Boston. As he was not spending any money and had yet to meet the elusive Master of the house, Thomas accepted the offer.

Having completed most of his notetaking, Thomas found time to look through the other library areas. It was incredible. There were at least a hundred volumes that could have netted a million dollars each, just resting on the shelves. He selected two or three volumes and set them on the coffee table. He wanted to read through them cover to cover. The knowledge of the Renaissance was contained in these books. One book in particular drew his attention: *Hero of Alexandra*. It was about a first-century inventor who made doors open automatically and statues move by using steam power.

As Thomas was sitting and reading by candlelight, the door opened, and a cloaked figure walked in wearing a carnival mask of the finest porcelain. The person had another cape and mask in hand. Thomas was startled for a moment before the figure spoke.

"Father, we must hurry. I have something wonderful to show you. But we must go right away...if you wish to see it." Thomas walked over to him, and he handed him the extra cloak and mask. "But we must go now, or your chance will be gone forever."

Not accustomed to such intrigue and yet relying on the comfort found within the villa, Thomas found himself trusting this figure. Aza had not moved from his spot lying next to him, which indicated he knew the scent of the person. Thomas got up, placing the cape around his shoulders, and securing the mask in place. Then, they headed down a winding staircase just off the foyer and onto a damp old walkway.

"Many of these houses had escape tunnels which were built at great expense—both money and human lives. We are about ten feet below the water level of Venice. The only thing holding out the water is the reinforced rock, rubble, dirt, and plaster used to build this path," the stranger explained as he moved ahead of Thomas while holding a glass-protected candle as their sole means of illumination.

The idea of dying like a rat in this sewer did nothing to calm Thomas's nerves, but to be beneath the ground in the underwater area of this city—a realm he had not even known existed—was thrilling. As Thomas followed his new companion, their footfalls reverberated around them. *We must look like two caped criminals fleeing in the night through the damp underworld.*

They entered St. Mark's Square through an old iron door; it took both men to push it open. After closing it back into place, Thomas turned to see the square filled with a sea of masks. The square was well known for such events, and this one appeared to be attended by thousands of people in costumes, swaying in dance to music that drowned out all other sounds.

"Here... down here, quickly," Thomas's companion called out, as he had started down a stairway leading below the Doge's Palace. Thomas followed without hesitation, and they were soon confronted by four large men in costumes of medieval Saracens. One of the men pushed a door open for them, and they ran through quickly, only to hear the door pulled closed behind them. They walked through another catacomb-like tunnel running the length of the palace above. They then turned and headed at a right angle north.

"Where are we?" Thomas finally asked.

"We are under the Bridge of Sighs," his companion whispered. As Thomas followed him, there was not a foot of distance between them. "They plan to renovate this section of the old prison starting next month." The stranger opened another door, and they walked into a cell area that held many distinguished visitors in its day. Thomas held his breath. "They find it too burdensome to keep it this way; they want to open it up to the tourists. But they will remove everything and make it look more like something Hollywood would dream up than what it was—a Hell on earth for the poor souls left down here to starve and die in the darkness."

He strode approximately twenty paces away from Thomas and stood at an open door. "Here, Father. Come and see for yourself."

Thomas walked up beside him, still overpowered by the gloom and depression of the setting. He wasn't quite sure how, but at that moment, he realized he was standing outside the cell that at one time housed Giordano Bruno. His guide handed him the candle lamp, as Thomas went into the small cell. Its walls were moist from seepage, and the smell of musk hung in the air. A wooden framed bed was adorned by a bit of moldy hay to sleep on, and beside it, sat a small desk with a chair. A copper chamber pot stood dully gleaming in the corner, and the stones of the wall glistened in the candle's lamplight. Thomas felt a form standing next to him, and for a moment, he was unaware his guide had also entered the room.

"This part of the dungeon was sealed off after they took Master Bruno out of here. They continued using the upper floors, but no one else was ever placed down here. The last person to occupy this room was Bruno himself." He spoke in a hushed tone as though his words might raise some specter.

"Look at this." He pointed to a Latin verse on the wall, carved by a human hand. Thomas lifted the lamp and read it aloud.

"THE UNIVERSE IS ALIVE, EVEN THOUGH I KNOW I AM ABOUT TO DIE." It was signed with the initials "G.B."

As Thomas held the candle up to get a closer inspection, he noticed etched in the wall just beneath the verse, was a picture depicting winged beings, throwing dark creatures through what looked like a doorway in the sky.

"What is this?" Thomas asked his masked colleague.

"That, my dear Father, is the reason you are here." The masked face looked directly at Thomas. "Now, we must go so as not to be found." The man took the candle from Thomas, then moved to the door and motioned to leave. "There are still those who don't want the truth ever to be known."

Thomas lingered another moment, looking from the wall to the pathetically tiny cell. He then turned to follow his guide back into the world above.

Ahead of him, Thomas could see the candlelight of his masked companion, weaving its way down the tunnels through which the two men had entered, and finally out through the steel door just beneath the Doge's Palace. As Thomas exited by way of the steel doorway and ventured up the stairs leading to St.

Mark's Square, he no longer saw the man. In front of him were hundreds of masked celebrators cavorting to the music, but the man had vanished just as quickly as he had arrived. Thomas removed his mask to get his bearings and then began his journey back to the villa. *The reason you are here,* continued racing through his mind.

Chapter 5

Dr. Lorenza Pellegrini took her seat in first class on Aer Lingus flight 7509 bound for Boston. After getting situated, she asked the flight attendant for a small glass of orange juice. From her purse, she removed two small white pills for her headache. Everything in her life was built on exactness. Having always loved reading other people's notes, she had limited her use of electronic devices in her world, in favor of a notebook to serve as a timekeeper and day scheduler. She carried a large leather book with her everywhere and recorded everything—dates, times, meetings, and outcomes. This, along with cryptic notes about the respective party involved—their personality, habits, and manners—for future reference. A single notebook would serve her for about a month; then, it would go up on the shelf in her office, and a new one started. That bookshelf in her office, represented the last ten years of her life, book by book.

She would only use a black fine-point pen to write with. Lorenza hated pencils with a deep and hostile passion. In her mind, pencils were designed for people who made mistakes in their thinking and writing. If she made a mistake, she wanted it right there in front of her, in black ink, so she could note it and work to make sure she did not commit the same error again.

Sitting there with her tray table down and her notebook open, she stared at the five names which now had thin black lines through them. She had scheduled meetings with each in the next two days, but now they all had to be postponed. Lorenza wore a gold and diamond Rolex on her left wrist and constantly looked at it when working. She noted the time she had called, who she had talked to, when she had rescheduled the appointment for, and any comments that might be relevant to future meetings. She had spent months negotiating with the Vatican to find a time and date that worked for two of the names on the list. Their time was so valuable she would most likely need to wait two additional months before having another opportunity to meet with them and get the four answers she needed from each of them. The other three names on her list did not matter since they needed her more than she needed them. They simply represented revenue. They needed her to authenticate some book or another, which they would then sell at auction if they had the real thing. A letter from her was like a gold seal of approval at any auction house in the world when it came to rare books. More times than not, she would have to deliver the news to some poor soul they had been duped and were now the owner of a high-grade forgery. It did not matter to her though; she still received her payment for services rendered. She wasn't cold about it—far from it. It was just business. She was passionate about books but hated the idea of someone producing a fake and claiming authority with it.

Lorenza looked up from her notebook to notice the older, silver-and-brown-haired man taking the seat next to her. His tanned face donning a pair of Bentley platinum and wood-framed glasses, coupled with his expensive three-piece suit and silk tie, made him look very dignified. While still handsome, Lorenza could only imagine what he must have looked like thirty years ago. A real head turner, she was sure. He politely nodded to her and pushed his old, brown, leather-worn briefcase under the seat in front of him. He sat down and placed his ticket back inside the left breast pocket of his coat, while taking it off and handing it to the flight attendant to hang in the first-class closet while in flight.

Lorenza looked again at where she was heading in the United States. Her full-time employer had sent a courier to her hotel with a detailed set of instructions. There had not been an 'oh by the way' or 'if you can when you have time.' The message had been direct as always— 'This needs to be done,' and nothing more. That was the reason why, for over the last ten years, she had taken to referring to him as her Master. She was not resentful, however. Everything she had acquired in the past decade was because of him. The circles she moved in were by his direction. The fortune she controlled in her name directly resulted from her relationship with him and him alone.

She had her own life, which was ancient books, and she could do whatever it was she wanted. There was no schedule for her. No one checked up on her. For her sake, the Master demanded everyone who dealt with her, do so with respect. He only added to her brilliance by providing opportunities few other scholars could ever obtain. Because of him, no door was ever barred to her. There was no glass ceiling in her world; she walked on top of it, and everyone that knew her was very aware of that fact. Attractiveness and beauty were just two of her apparent qualities. Her mind was the real prize, containing an encyclopedic-like knowledge of medieval and renaissance literature, books, printers, and a keen awareness of those striving to destroy that same knowledge.

Lorenza was more curious about why this round of instructions was nearly identical to those she received from the Vatican just hours prior.

Something she would need to reconcile in the next few days.

As she looked around the cabin preparing for takeoff, she noticed the man next to her had both hands gripping the armrests tightly. His knuckles were white from the strain. Lorenza leaned over and said, "Here, hold my hand. You are afraid of flying; it would seem." She was now looking directly into his face. His mild gray eyes met hers, and he interlocked one of his hands into one of hers.

"It is a ploy to get beautiful women to take sympathy on me." He smiled, but it didn't reach his eyes and lines of stress fanned from their corners.

"I highly doubt that." She patted their intertwined hands with her other. As the aircraft accelerated, it moved quickly and smoothly into the air as the view out the window revealed the receding city below them.

The man took a deep breath and let it out slowly. He then gradually removed his hand from hers and leaned toward her to speak. "I hate takeoffs and landings. I have since I was a young child. Once we are in the air, it is a wonderful feeling to look down on the earth like angels do." He sat back in his seat and crossed his hands over his flat abdomen.

Lorenza felt a warmth from him, like someone she had known before somewhere. She let the thought drift and went back to her notebook. In just a few minutes, they were over the Tyrrhenian Sea, heading north by west. For the next eleven hours, this would be Lorenza's office, inside this aircraft.

47

They claimed it took that long to go from Rome to Boston but going west in the northern hemisphere always took longer, since the headwinds pushed against aircraft. It would more likely take twelve hours or even thirteen if they were backed up at Logan Airport in Boston. Half a day spent sitting. Not Lorenza's idea of time well spent.

Somewhere over the Atlantic Ocean, after lunch had been served, Lorenza pulled out a book she had in her shoulder bag. Her companion had skipped lunch altogether and worked at editing several printed sheets, now and then mumbling, and shaking his head with disconcertment. What he was reading was clearly upsetting to him. She took the lambskin wrapping off the old book, placed it down on the table before her, and picked up where she had most recently left off.

About ten minutes into her reading, she noticed the man next to her abruptly stop and click his mechanical pencil, causing the lead to retract inside.

"I am sorry to be a bore, but I must ask why such a bright young woman like you is reading that piece of rubbish." He placed his pencil down on the stack of papers and turned to her. "Vasari was a cheat, a liar, a thief, and most everything he knew was from the stories he picked up in the taverns and public houses."

Lorenza felt as though someone had hit her in the gut. *How did he know what she was reading? How could he possibly know what she was reading?*

"You know this book?" She asked.

48

"Of course. It's Giorgio Vasari's biography of Leonardo. He wrote it with two Inquisition members standing over him to make sure he did not say anything that would suggest Leonardo was anything but a good practicing Catholic, with the highest regard toward the Church." A hint of color that hadn't been present since take-off, climbed in his cheeks. "Good grief, Vasari makes him sound like some monk living in a cave and glorifying God with all his art. The work of Girolamo Savonarola, the Dominican, was much more accurate, yet the Church went out of its way to make sure it never saw the light of day." He shook his head, his eyes bright as he spoke. "To believe Vasari, one would think DaVinci was completely asexual with no physical desires whatsoever. Savonarola spoke openly about DaVinci's love of Jacopo Saltarello, the prostitute, who had a wild affair with the greatest man alive at the time. It was only the intervention by the Medici that kept Leonardo from ending up being fried in the town square in a bonfire." He sat sideways in his chair and folded his hands. "Who are you if I may ask?

"Dr. Lorenza Pellegrini, from Venice, and you are..." Lorenza sat up, ready for a confrontation.

"Professor Ritter Von Troppen, University of Buenos Aires, Chair of the Department of Historical Studies specializing in the Renaissance period of Florence." He paused. "Dr. Lorenza Pellegrini. I do know of you. 'The wrecker of dreams,' I once heard

49

you referred to as." He smiled again at her, and Lorenza found it charming.

"Wrecker of dreams?" She asked puzzled.

"You're the young lady who tells people they have fake books and forgeries. Delano San Augustine hates you with a passion beyond compare." He laughed.

"Oh no, you know him?" Lorenza was in disbelief. *What are the odds?* She had destroyed San Augustine's belief he had an authentic set of letters from Caravaggio during his exile from Rome.

"He had gone to maybe three or four other scholars, less well known than you. None of them would commit, but equally, none of them came right out and told him the letters were done almost a hundred years after Caravaggio was dead, either." Again, he chuckled. "He thought he had gotten a good deal on them from some kind old lady in Florence who was ignorant of their value. That was his story anyway. He gave her two thousand Euros for them and laughed all the way back to Paraguay. Then, after three years of trying to get them authenticated by anyone with a reputation, he found you, and all his plans involving a life of style and comfort came crumbling down around him." He paused and asked the flight attendant for two glasses of red wine. Lorenza closed the book, re-wrapped it, and placed it back into her shoulder bag.

"I cannot make out your accent. May I ask, what is your native tongue?" Lorenza took the wine, and they clinked glasses.

"My first language was German. My family had migrated to Argentina long before the first world war. We were in the shipping business."

"So, your second language is Spanish, I would imagine?" she asked him.

"Yes, and Italian is my fifth. I get by, but not as well as I would like to, since my mind still speaks inside my head in Spanish, as you can imagine. How many languages, may I ask, do you speak?" He sipped at his wine.

"Four, in addition to reading Latin and Greek." Her cheeks warmed at the white lie. She could speak both but avoided admitting it at the risk of sounding pretentious.

"The short paragraph on the back of your last book left a lot to be desired in getting to know anything about you. I must say, I had this vision of an older woman with gray mop-like hair, stuffed away in some dusty corner of a library basement, chain-smoking, speaking in a gravelly voice, and wearing large, coke-bottle glasses." Again, he paused, "I took it upon myself to find out what I could about you. Your work impresses me greatly, and your scholarship appears impeccable. But as I looked through social media, in the journals, and then even in more arcane places, I discovered I could find very little on you. It was like an object in the mist. There, but just out of sight." He studied her with unwavering focus.

"Is this the place where you ask me to tell you about myself?" She beamed a big smile at him. "Because that is my least favorite subject to discuss."

"Indulge me. I am a good listener and would love to know more about the infamous Dr. Lorenza Pellegrini. Be kind to this nice older man; we clearly have the time, since we are still hours away from Boston. And I would much rather hear your voice than read this trash I have been tasked with peer review." He touched the pages on the table in front of him.

"Alright. But understand, trust comes hard for me. I don't want to see this published next month in *People* magazine under your by-line." She tossed her head and laughed, finding herself enjoying the interaction.

"I promise. Perhaps just a quick letter to Delano telling him what a charming companion I had during a recent flight while letting slip who it was, with some glowing remarks about you." His grin was almost evil.

"Oh, you are bad. I was born in Milan, an only child. Father was, or should I say still is, an architect. Mother was a teacher. She was killed by a drunk driver when I was very young. I don't remember her at all. Just nothing at all." Lorenza drifted off with that thought for a moment. "My father was struggling in his business, as he was just beginning, and I was a burden he didn't know what to do with. His twin brother Roberto in Florence was much more established and settled. He, too, was an architect but had taken a job with the city to remodel and restore older buildings. So, he had a good income—a nice little house with a great view of the river—and a comfortable lifestyle. He told my father I should come and live with him and his girlfriend for a year until things improved in Milan. I spent the next sixteen years there. They got married when I was about five, and then we were just a family unit. She became a sort of mother to me as well as a good friend. Neither she, nor my uncle ever told me not to do anything. They forced me to grow up knowing for myself what was right and wrong. They always had guidance for me, but I had to ask for it." Lorenza took a sip of her wine and asked her travel companion, "am I boring you yet?"

"Not in the slightest," Von Troppen responded. "Please, go on."

"Roberto had a passionate hatred for the Church. So, I was not sent to Catholic school as a child. He enrolled me in a private school for gifted children, which taught us how to be better, more intellectual, and more open to the world of possibilities. When my childhood peers from the neighborhood were going through their different phases, I was always watching them and secretly laughing at them behind their backs. It is pretty strange to think about now. I knew a lot of them but was never really part of them." Lorenza drifted again and looked out the window for a moment at the sea below them.

"Roberto was a bit of a conspiracy theorist. He read everything dealing with the group. He had one book, *Holy Blood Holy Grail*. An older book he had highlighted, underlined, marked with comments, and stuck extra notes in. It was almost like a bible to him. Everything else in his library was of the same vein. I read it to see what held his mind to these feelings. I enjoyed it so much, I too, became hooked. I read everything he had, and then began buying similar books. Everything I said ended in a question mark. I started to infuriate my teachers as well as the other students in high school. Nothing was sacred to me, as I questioned everything and constantly queried what the underlying motivation behind this or that was."

The flight attendant came by and refilled both of their glasses. The two cheered their glasses again, and Von Troppen motioned for her to proceed.

"I started University when I was seventeen. Now I had a whole new group of victims to subject my views to." Lorenza laughed at the memory. "I was a literature major, with plans of being a schoolteacher in some place away from the city. That was until I met Umberto, an upper-division lit. professor. Young, maybe twenty-eight, but already a flame under everyone's backside. A communist, radical, demonstrator...handsome, brilliant, dangerous, and street tough. A true force with which to be reckoned." Lorenza grinned.

"It started with an argument in a bistro one night over whether the Priory of Sion was real or not.

For every argument I made, he had a comeback and whatever else, that stopped me in my tracks. I found between school, reading all the books he recommended to me on the side, and spending time with him, I hardly slept at all. I spent entire nights at his place reading philosophy, ethics, hermetics, alchemy, modern thought, Eastern theology, books by people that were clearly mad, and some by people that *should* have gone insane. He constantly enquired if I had gotten the hidden meaning in them and, if not, why not. Words—*all* words—took on different flavors and significance to me.

My other classes were a joke. I was whizzing through them, and in a few, it was clear I had a greater command of the subject than the person teaching the course. In my humble opinion." Lorenza chuckled, the wine causing a warm glow to spread through her. "A few of my writings for some of these classes bordered on the edge of masterpieces. One of my professors instructed me not to come back to class after reading my paper. He said I was being passed with the highest mark possible and acknowledged he had nothing to teach me.

"Before I moved in with him, he required two things from me. First, I needed Roberto and Julia's permission, and secondly, I could not leave school for any reason until after I had graduated. Getting Julia's buy-in was easy. She understood, and then proceeded to help smooth the path for my uncle's buy-in as well. He still did so reluctantly." Lorenza paused for a moment. "I have not spoken this much about my life in years. Yet it seems like yesterday."

"Please don't stop; I am truly fascinated." He motioned for the flight attendant to refill his glass. Lorenza's was still full. He then requested her to proceed.

Lorenza obliged. "I moved in, and once the reality of passion was mixed with the heady world of knowledge, it was one constant battle after another to see who was the smartest, sharpest, and quickest in... everything. A quiet evening with jazz on the stereo and a couple of glasses of cheap wine and an argument about heresy could explode between us.

"One night, the police showed up inquiring about all the screaming. I told them Umberto was defending Martin Luther's points as self-serving and I was claiming he was supporting the laymen against the misuse of power by the Church. The two officers looked at each other and then asked us if this Luther fellow was around so they could talk to him. We both broke out laughing.

"It should come as no surprise, or maybe it should, we drifted apart during my fourth year of university, and I settled into my own place. I was preparing for graduate school. It had been both wonderful and terrible. Graduate school was like a trade school. You learn the same things as at the university, only more in-depth. I walked through it to a Doctorate and then realized the dreams of teaching were now long dead ghosts.

"I started my first 'real job' at a museum in Florence, working in special collections, as a reviewer of fine books they were interested in purchasing, but unsure whether they had value or not. By this time, I had twenty binders of notes and could trace a publisher down within minutes, as well as know everything they had ever published within an hour. I rejected hundreds of forgeries and fakes. Then arriving at the post one day, I received two books from a person in Venice. They had no desire to sell them; they wanted me to authenticate them and write reviews. Looking back now, I realize it was a job interview, but at the time, I was completely unaware of the fact.

"It took about a week for each. They were extraordinarily complex, rare, and magnificent manuscripts written by hand. I spent ten to twelve hours a day working on them. Everything about them, paper, ink, language, structure, grammar, punctuation, watermarks, the covers, the leather, the gold embossment on them. The thread that was used to assemble them. It took me another two weeks to write up the evaluation documents. I measured every word I used, to make sure I had not understated nor overstated anything about them. I copied one of them by hand for myself. The content was magnificent, and the person that wrote it was off the scale in terms of insight, brilliance, and understanding. He was espousing ideas centuries ahead of his time.

"When I had finished the project, I cried for an hour. Probably never again would I have such an opportunity to look inside the mind of a pure genius and see how he perceived the world four hundred years ago. I needed to read everything ever published by him or about him. Giordano Bruno became my new fascination and love." Lorenza stopped and smiled, now slightly embarrassed by her last comment and apparent ramblings. "All of this was more than you anticipated, I imagine." She smiled awkwardly and sipped her wine.

"Not at all. Anyone who has ever read Master Bruno, knows all knowledge exists both in this time and in some time still yet to come." The older man had an immediate grasp on what she had always felt. "So, what occurred next?"

"That was just over ten years ago. The person who sent those books to me, called me and offered to set me up in business. A consultant in rare and unusual books for major libraries, universities, museums, and private collectors. All expenses paid for three offices, one in Rome, Florence, and his home in Venice, where he had ten thousand rare books in need of proper cataloging and abstracts written about many of them. He told me he would cover all the expenditures and pay me a yearly stipend. He would also direct business to me. I did not consider the offer for very long and was particularly curious as to what would happen. So, I said yes. The rest is, as they say, history, and I have now worked for him for the last decade—the national libraries of six European nations, ten major auction houses, and hundreds of private collectors. I am on call at the Vatican, which is essentially why I am on this flight. I have a potentially priceless book to look at in Boston. Now it is your turn, Herr Doktor Professor." She smiled at him and sat back, ready to listen.

His story was as fascinating as her own, and Lorenza found herself taken in by the details. Not long after he had concluded, the flight attendant's voice echoed through the overhead speakers, informing the passengers to replace their tray tables and return their chairs into the upright and locked positions. They were coming into Boston a half-hour earlier than expected.

After the flight, they exchanged business cards and told each other they needed to keep in contact. Upon disembarking, Lorenza hugged him as he did her, and then they both went their separate ways. After collecting her bag from claim carousel four, Lorenza pulled out her leather notebook. She looked at the name she had written down in preparation for her trip, along with the one-word description accompanying it. *Father Albert Kennedy: Exorcist.*

Chapter 6

Night had closed in around the old house that sat on the coast of Massachusetts. It was said to have been built by a whaling captain who never got the chance to see it completed. The captain's wife had moved into it while he was away in the Pacific hunting humpbacks. He was overdue home by two months, when word came from another whaler informing her the captain would not be returning home again. Locals had often told the story she lived in the house for the next fifty years and stepped out of it just once in all that time, which was when a friend took her to the local hospital where she died.

Over the years, four different families owned it. All of them experiencing some type of tragedy in their lives while living there. Or at least that is the story Dr. David Wright was told after he had purchased the home, and finally moved in a little over three years ago. The locals were concerned he would fall befouled of some misfortune inhabiting the house. David just laughed it off. Moving there and buying the place had been a dream of his for many years, and no stories of ghosts or misty apparitions on the staircase were going to drive him away. Besides, David had already experienced what he considered actual evil during his fifteen years of practice as a psychoanalyst in Boston, most of which had been done by humans to other humans.

David had bought the place with the royalties from the first book he published, which dealt with the psychological aspects of possessions and exorcisms. It had been a best-seller, yet most people hated it, for it removed a lot of the mystery from the event and gave a fair amount of valid reasoning and psychological understanding to the whole enterprise. What David found more surprising though, was the fact the Catholic Church appeared to endorse it.

The power had gone out about thirty minutes prior, as the evening's storm coming straight off the sea was proving to be a strong one. Even with all the renovations, the old house still moaned in howling winds. David loved it. *What a great setting for ghost stories*. However, the only thing haunting his place tonight was his old Labrador retriever with the arthritic leg, Ralph. David had named him when he brought him home from the shelter. Not Socky, Yeller, or some other ridiculous name, but Ralph— or Raf, the European version. Ralph was David's watchdog, and he was quite sure if someone broke into this place, Ralph would do his best to drive them off after he licked them to death while leaving a coat of his hair all over them.

Ralph had come up the steps, staggered into the bedroom, and climbed upon the bed, which he was never supposed to do. Or at least that is what David had told him when he first brought him home. Since then, those rules vanished along with all the other ones, which typically happens to rules when those truly caring about animals are involved in their enforcement. He ate human food with David; he especially liked pizza. He was known to dig through the trash can and forage for leftovers or tear up the cardboard from discarded paper towel rolls when left by himself for too long. Most nights, he would not come upstairs after he was settled down on the couch or a chair in the living room. Tonight though, it was the storm that brought him upstairs. Ralph did not like storms. He especially disliked the lightning and thunder often accompanying them. Ralph wasn't a runner; he was a hider. He had already forced his head under the coverlet on the bed and was curled up beneath it when the cell phone vibrated on the nightstand. David fumbled to grab his phone and answered, "Hello?"

"Hello, David? It's Father Graham," announced the voice on the other end of the phone. Father Benjamin Graham was the Abbot and Chancellor of All Saints College in Boston. Over the years, David had come to know Father Graham, and while he and David were well-acquainted, he would not consider them friends. David's work with Graham's colleague at the college, Father Albert Kennedy, or *The Exorcist* as he was referred to in certain circles, prevented that from occurring.

"Father, is everything alright?" David pulled the phone from his ear quickly to see the time reflecting 12:15 a.m. and immediately knew the answer.

"I have some sad news as well as a request requiring your immediate attention, if you have the time right now to hear it." Father Graham spoke politely; however, David knew Graham didn't care whether the time was good or not.

"Go ahead, Father." David braced himself, as all the normal ideations ran through his brain. *Kennedy's sick. Kennedy's in the hospital. Kennedy had a complete mental collapse because of his work.*

"David, Father Kennedy killed himself yesterday." Graham let the words sink in for a moment before proceeding. "He also left a note."

"A note?" David inquired.

"A suicide note, it appears," Graham stated. "In it, he requested you handle everything for him. As you know, he had no family, and due to these circumstances, we cannot now be of service to him. We are forbidden from providing him with a mass, dealing with his body, or finding a place to bury him. Even though he requested you have him cremated, I would pray you would reconsider the request. At Last Judgment, he would still want his chance for redemption, I would imagine." Graham was old school. Suicides were terrible enough, but for a priest to break from God was unthinkable in his mind, and the Church equally shared the outlook. He added, "Father Kennedy left certain things for you in a sealed box. I am required to tell you if there is anything within the box involving the Church, you must return it to us. All of his files are being packed up now, and they will be shipped to the Diocese Office of the Bishop and will then be forwarded to Rome for filing."

What a waste of valuable information, David thought. His files were a treasure trove for a researcher. Thirty-five years of dealing in the darkness of the human mind and finding methods to return someone's life to them through exorcism was unbelievable. Now those files would become damp, dirty, rat-eaten, and covered with mold over the next five years in the basement of the Vatican. *That would not have been what Kennedy wanted for them.*

Kennedy was one of the most open men with whom David had ever dealt. If asked a question, Kennedy could answer and then back it up with case studies he had done over the years. Their relationship had grown from a collaboration years ago, working with a single patient of David's, into a deep-rooted friendship based on mutual respect for one another, both professionally and personally. Over the past three years, Kennedy had been up to David's house often, many times talking well into the morning about all things paranormal. Before anything else though, Kennedy was a scientist of the first tier. He never fell back on dogma to hold a position in a discussion. If Kennedy was unfamiliar or did not know something, he would make that fact very clear. But, if he was certain, neither heaven nor Earth could change his mind. Kennedy respected Einstein's work as much as he did kabbalistic teachings, lessons of which he had taken from a Rabbi in Boston, largely to the irritation of the Church. "Can someone pick me up at the train station this afternoon?" David asked in a solemn voice.

"Of course, David. Just call my office when you are about to arrive, and someone will be there. Thank you, David, for understanding. I will see you this afternoon." The phone line went dead. It appeared Graham wanted to quickly wash his hands of this matter to get on with other more important things. Priests who quit and those who offed themselves were not held in high esteem by the managers of the Church.

David looked out the window at the occasional flashes of light tearing through the night sky and considered what he needed to pack for his trip back to Boston.

Jeans and sweaters were not the appropriate clothing for dealing with the dead.

Chapter 7

The morning light seemed to come early into Thomas's upstairs room. Recalling the previous night's events, brought on an overwhelming rush of emotions seeming to get the better of him. Thomas felt he needed to find his guide and thank him for taking him to the Palace and also, to inquire what he meant by his final words to him.

As Thomas surveyed his room, he abruptly remembered it was Sunday, and he wanted to take in an early service at one of the smaller churches away from the center of the city's activities. He had an intense yearning to be amongst the people who lived on these islands. Thomas did not wish to participate, but merely observe the congregation during Mass. In preparation, he donned the new soft clothes, which now, over the past few days, he had grown accustomed to wearing, and left the villa to walk towards the small church off of one of the nearby piazzas. Carlos was already up and shining the chrome on the boat as Thomas came out onto the landing. At the end of the dock was a small footpath leading to the street by a bridge. From there, it was a short walk to the church.

"Good morning, Carlos." Thomas stopped for a moment and watched the care Carlos was taking to keep this boat looking so pristine.

"Good morning, Father. Did you have a restful evening last night?" He looked up and smiled at Thomas.

"Not really...but I would like to thank whoever it was who took me on my nocturnal journey," Thomas replied.

"Pardon, Father?" Carlos stood up straight after rubbing a chrome strip and used the same cloth to wipe his hands. He gazed back at Thomas with a relatively blank stare. "Who are you talking about?"

"The visitor from last night. The man in the costume who took me to the carnival." Thomas stared at Carlos' now-questioning face as it showed surprise.

"Father, I know of no one who came into the manor last night. Besides, there was no carnival last night. You would have heard the fireworks. They are so noisy here in the small back alleys." Carlos shrugged his shoulders and went back to rubbing on a piece of chrome.

Thomas waited for a moment and then took his leave. He headed down in the direction of the small square where the church was located. Puzzled as he was right now, Thomas decided to resolve this circumstance later in the day. Walking along the small street, he was surprised as his thoughts turned to the possibility last night's experience had all been a dream. *How else can I explain such an adventure?* The question of his sanity also occurred to him, and yet he felt more in touch with himself than he had in years. He crept into the chilly darkness of the church and could see the heads of those who were already in their pews awaiting the arrival of the processional. Taking a seat in the rear of the church, Thomas sat reflecting further on what had happened the night before. Was it just a dream after all? Something had occurred, but now he was not sure what.

After Mass had ended and the faithful had left, Thomas continued to sit in the back of the church in quiet contemplation. He let his thoughts drift to his book. Thomas knew it was time to start compiling his notes for its completion. It would take just a few more weeks to bring it all together and reach the conclusion he desired. He wanted complete vindication for Master Bruno, and nothing less felt appropriate. Thomas had never considered himself a man of compulsion, but this discovery of the lost texts and the framework in which they placed his work, was at least as relevant today as it was in his own time. Bruno was a philosopher who should take his rightful place on the top shelf next to Plato and Aristotle; he'd understood exobiology and cosmology as well as any modern scientist.

Thomas suddenly realized a tall man in a suit had sat down next to him on the pew. He did not remember seeing this man when he looked over the congregation earlier. Thomas noticed the man was praying silently. After crossing himself, he turned to Thomas and stared intensely into his eyes. Thomas observed the man's eyes were a pale blue, and his face looked tanned and leather-lined with age, yet he seemed young and strong in figure and form.

"Father, I must ask you to discontinue your quest. It will be harmful to you and others if you do not drop this matter and find other fields to plow." Thomas found his speech quaint and distinct, with just a slight accent in his Italian. "You cannot serve two masters. The choice is yours...but the next time they will send someone more prone to action than I."

"What are you talking about?" Thomas gazed at him, eyes narrowed. "How do you know I am a priest?"

"I read people's souls like ink on parchment. Leave this place, for no good will come of your presence here." He got up and walked out of the church without another word.

It took Thomas a moment to collect his thoughts. He then followed the man into the sunlight outside, and while shading his eyes, he tried to find his figure in the crowd of people passing by. He was nowhere to be seen. *This is becoming a common theme.*

His threat cut through Thomas like something tangible. He shuddered even though he stood in the bright warm sunshine. *They will send someone more prone to action than I.* Thomas repeated it over and over, out loud to himself. *What did he mean? Whom have I offended so profoundly?*

"Are you all right, my son?" The older priest who had performed the Mass was now standing next to Thomas.

"Yes, Padre. I was trying to find the man who was sitting beside me just now in the pew." Thomas turned again and surveyed the crowd but did not see him or anyone who looked like him.

"I saw you sitting in the back of the Church by yourself. There was no one next to you, Father." The older man put a hand on Thomas's shoulder. "Perhaps you were mistaken. Would you care to have a glass of cold iced tea with me in the garden?"

Thomas turned again and looked directly into the man's face. With a kind and gentle smile, the priest started to lead Thomas along with him. "We don't get very many other priests coming around here, nor do we see very many tourists. You may wonder how I know you are a priest? That is simple. You were mouthing the words I normally speak at the altar. Most of my parishioners could not do that. The absence of jewelry except for a fine watch, coupled with the nature of your clothing, tells an old man a lot. You were not with a family, and you sought the shelter of the back of the church. Add that up, and you have either a criminal with morals or a priest who is not wanting to be recognized." He led Thomas to a small door at the side of the church, which opened onto a formal garden with an abundance of shade trees.

"How delightful this is," Thomas gasped. The small garden featured plenty of roses along with its trees. The priest led him over to a spot where they could sit under a large tree. He sat down while folding his robe in front of Thomas.

"So, which is it?" The priest smiled and nodded his thanks to an older woman who brought out some iced tea on a platter and placed it between them. She returned the nod and went back to the portico where she had been watching and working.

"Which is what, Father?"

"A priest or a criminal? What kind of man am I entertaining in my garden?" He sipped his iced tea and wiped his mouth carefully.

Thomas laughed and picked up his drink. The glass felt cold, and the tea had the color of wheat harvested late in summer. He drank half a glassful before he realized it. "A little of both, I am sure. But I'm certain you already know I am a priest. I am here researching a new book. I am hoping to have it published."

"A scholar? A dangerous thing, being a scholar in Venice. Many have been here over the years and have found scholarship and faith do not always go hand in hand." He leaned back and let the filtered sunlight play across his face. "Most people do not know Venice was built on the souls of the damned. Greed, corruption, and deceit were the midwives of this city. People speak of London, Paris, or New York as representing all that is temporal in this world, but the true heart of this world is here and always has been. These canals have seen the greatest and worst men from Western history float down them. The great masked balls held here were the stages for Demigods and Demons to meet openly and play their tricks on unsuspecting humans while slaves chained in galley ships rowed potentates from Asia to Venice. Their purpose was only to see the rare pale flesh of European women. The rectory where I sleep, was once home for a Moorish prince from North Africa. He kept a harem of more than twenty women here and smoked hashish from a water pipe. He bought and sold humans like loaves of bread. The Church Fathers looked the other way because he built all this for them. Each stone in this floor represents someone's life in bondage." He paused as his hand gestured around him. "Oh, listen to me...I sound like some old man who has nothing better to talk about than what the neighbors are doing."

"No. It is fine, Father. I am truly interested. Since I have been here, I have seen several things my mind keeps telling me should not be. But they are." Thomas found himself warming to the older man.

"This is a dream-world, halfway between everything else. Many things here are not as they should be. But most of the tourists miss it, and fewer

75

and fewer people live in the city anymore because of it. Many of the villas and houses are empty. They are now only filled with the memories and ghosts of what once existed." Novelli stared at Thomas intensely. "However, if you stay too long, you will start to see things not as they are but how you would like them to be. That is addictive to most. It happens over a long period for some, but in others, this habit quickly attaches itself, and they are caught up in things not of this world or the next." He got up and straightened his alb. "Please excuse me now. I need to start my rounds of the sick in the area. Most are old and fearing their next journey, so I need to go and assure them it will be wonderful. Please feel free to sit here and enjoy yourself. It would be nice if we could have dinner and spend an evening together. I would love to hear about your book. But I would advise you as a friend you might want to consider going to Florence or Verona to finish it. The air here becomes too intoxicating for scholars sometimes." He smiled again and picked up his breviary.

"I should like that as well, Father. Who should I ask for at the rectory?" Thomas stood and shook his old hand.

"Novelli. Father Bertinaro Novelli. Good day, my brother. Hold onto this for me until next time we meet."

He walked back into the church, and Thomas stood there for a few moments considering all he had said, not yet looking down at the leather pouch. Looking now to inspect the small bag, Thomas opened it and found inside an elegant silver crucifix and chain. It was ancient and ornate, and the detail was incredible. He put it in his pocket and left via the Judas gate on the side of the garden, re-emerging into the world of people going about their daily business. As Thomas walked through the late afternoon sun, his mind replayed the events with the man in the pew and Father Novelli's words.

Chapter 8

Upon Thomas' return to the villa, everything was quiet. He expected such, considering it was Sunday and all the workers in the house had the day off. A candle was burning in the foyer, and there was a lamp there for Thomas' use. In his room, Thomas opened the wooden shutters to let in the night air and sat by the window looking at the lights moving around the canal and the city. He took the small crucifix from his pocket and studied it. Something about the crucifix was fascinating to him. He was not sure if it was the design or structure, but holding it caused a certain feeling to come over him. It was a strange experience; he couldn't grasp exactly why, but it had something to do with sense, texture, vibrations.

Sitting by the window, Thomas began to consider and reflect upon the past few days. He had not seen a newspaper, watched television, or listened to a radio. He had witnessed things that had never occurred to him before: like a leopard being a pet in someone's house; seeing Bruno's cell; and witnessing a festival that had supposedly not occurred. Then, there were people talking to him who were not there; and others who were holding books that should not exist. His compulsion to solve the mystery of Bruno's manuscripts – an issue of significance only to a handful of scholars in the world — had caused the days to merge into one. Much of his research had been vainglorious on his part. Thomas had seen it as essential to contribute to the collective knowledge of humankind in his humble manner. Still, in reflection, he realized much of what he had done was only to prove his theory correct and to prove others wrong. Bruno had become the center of his universe and the hub from which all the spokes of his life had extended outward. The isolation he had imposed upon himself was something he had worn as a badge of honor, though it meant forsaking a life intertwined with other humans on a truly personal basis.

He had become a good instructor, a fair scholar, and a fine researcher, but his role as a priest and his inner devotion to his Church was something he suddenly began to consider in a different light. The vocation of faith was not his strong suit. He accepted the tenets of the faith without question, but he found he had used his role as a way of avoiding being involved in life. Thomas had even given up executing Mass daily and substituted a simple prayer in the morning. He felt it would suffice for the needs and responsibilities he had accepted when he took his mantle twenty-one years ago. Father Novelli's practice of making rounds to the sick within his parish to offer comfort seemed alien to him. *And yet, was that not a priest's role in life?*

Thomas had spent his time the past five years formulating his attack on the central establishment of the Church, specifically surrounding the Renaissance. *But why? To vindicate a man who was long dead but read about today? Is this desire for him or myself?* Thomas did not like the implications of that question. Father Pierre Teilhard de Chardin had written volumes in the nineteen twenties on evolutionary biology and human paleontology only to have the Holy See forbid him from publishing them. He did not bend to this prohibition yet remained within the arms of the Church. When published twenty years later, his books were hallmarks for all who came after him in the fields of philosophy and anthropology. *If the Ecumenical Council placed the same injunction on my work, could I stand to remain within the Church, or would I leave to see it published within my lifetime? Would I be willing for the sake of truth to accept the label of heretic and turn from all I have known in my*

81

adult life behind? If so, Thomas would have to try to find out what it would be like to be just another person in a world filled with people. *Could I embrace the silence imposed by those who have not done the work that I have accomplished and accept the decision of those I saw as lesser scholars judging my work?* Thomas felt his world both collapsing and exploding around him simultaneously. He sat wondering if there was a middle ground that would allow him to retain his position and still publish his works.

Ignorance is bliss, he thought. *Only someone truly intelligent could come up with such an adage. Ignorance is usually wrapped in monochromatic arrogance, seeing only black and white and not allowing for grays of a thousand shades. The Church once executed dissenters for believing the earth was not the center of the universe or the earth was not flat. Bruno thought there were other worlds having multiple shapes and sizes and a variety of intelligent life. It is much like trying to resolve relativity and quantum physics. The main question is, how could Bruno be so sure he was right in all his declarations? Did he have a glimpse into the workings of the universe others had not realized? Commitment or consecration, knowledge or belief – that was and still is the question.*

Thomas dressed in his Romans and left the villa quietly. He walked to St. Mark's Square and looked out at the prison from the Bridge of Sighs. Thomas wanted to get back into the jail and see the prison cell before it was destroyed forever. Walking along the front of the Doge's Palace, he tried every door. Only a few tourists lingered in the square now, and no one seemed to notice the solitary priest. Thomas finally found the staircase, but it was blocked off at the bottom by an iron, padlocked gate. He was not sure what he wanted, but it seemed to him he would have a connection to the truth if he could find the cell again. Thomas descended the stairs and shook the gate with all his strength, hoping to open it, but all it did was make a noise. When he looked up, he saw only faces of a man and woman looking down at him. They were wearing the uniforms of the Constabulary of Venice.

"Father, what are you doing down there?" the woman asked him.

"I was trying to break into the Palace to see the dungeon. I need to see it tonight." Thomas walked back up the steps, holding the hem of his robe.

"Padre, it is closed. Normal visiting hours are in the daytime. Come back tomorrow, and you can take the tour." She added, concerned, "It is very late for a priest to be out, Padre. Can we escort you home?"

"No. Forgive me. I was just overcome with a desire I cannot explain. I did not notice the time." His excuse seemed absurd, but Thomas did not know what else to say.

"Will you be alright, or should we call someone?" The young man observed him, and Thomas realized he had overstepped a boundary and would not be wise to continue.

Thomas regained some of his composure. "No, thank you. I can make it fine. I will walk along the waterfront and let the sea air clear my head. Thank you for your concern."

The woman touched his arm. "It is late, Padre, and I would feel better if we escorted you home. I don't want to see anything happen to you."

"Thank you, my dear. But I am fine. Please forgive my actions. I just wanted to see one thing and thought I could inspect it without being noticed." Thomas forced a smile and then nodded.

They both touched their caps and walked on, leaving him there to find his way back. His response had not been subtle, but at least they respected the clothing enough to allow him freedom of movement. *I guess I will have to work through this problem on my own*. Thomas decided to walk the long way back to the villa. So much had happened, and he needed to sort through all the thoughts flooding his mind.

As he walked through the back streets and small alleys of the sleeping city, Thomas was moved by the sense something else was happening around him; exactly what, he was not sure. Thomas knew he needed to avoid the conditional reflex of someone confronted with a world turning fantastic in front of them: passing off strange occurrences as synchronicity or an overactive imagination. Still, Thomas had this nagging sensation something just below the surface connected all these events.

As a modern man, Thomas thought of himself as a realist. The needs of reality governed his behavior, and he suspected this habit might be the crux of the problem. Concepts of good and evil have generally been reduced to the bounds of human behavior even within the confines of the Church. The various Orders of the Church have worked to expunge evil as a supernatural force and have relegated it to the deeds of man.

He stopped in front of an antique refurbishing shop. Through the window, Thomas saw pieces of furniture hundreds of years old being re-crafted by a master who could make them look like new, even though they were as ancient as this city. Thomas began to realize his belief in the faith had faded and become obscured behind the scholarship. *It is a razor's edge which all of us walk.* We have no proof of existence beyond this life, we must have faith. But faith is the first thing challenged when confronted with the supernatural. Try as he might for logic, Thomas knew all the incidents happening to him recently were not in the standard order of things. Books out of time and place, people who knew more about him than he did himself...he was trusting the words of strangers without question. All of this was an alien landscape. The reason for his acceptance was simple; he wanted to finish his book and prove he was right and the rest of the world was wrong.

Thomas paid close attention to the sound of his footfalls on the cobblestone alley. The walkways were mainly dark, except with the occasional lamplight. *If gas lamps replaced the electrical lights, this alley would look no different than it did in Bruno's day.* The cool sea air surrounded him, and he felt a chill. Thomas stopped in his tracks to listen to the sounds around him. There was no movement, but Thomas had an uneasy feeling something or someone was out there — he just felt it. He knew he could run back to the main street where there would be more light and maybe even a few people but running did not seem to be the right option.

When he was in seminary, he boxed and was good at it. He enjoyed the fights in the ring, and even though it had been twenty years since he had last laced a glove on his hand, his skills and physical prowess had not left him. He resumed walking, noting his surroundings, glancing into the shadows where someone might be lurking or waiting for an unsuspecting victim.

Suddenly, out of nowhere, Thomas heard a voice in the shadows behind him, "Father, forgive me for what I must do." The voice was low and basso.

Thomas quickly turned and saw the man with lengthy brown hair and a long dark cloak draped around his shoulders. His eyes shone like stars.

Thomas told him, "I wish not to hurt you, my son, but one step closer, and I shall teach you the litany of the step, jab, and punch." Thomas stood perfectly still, looking on as the man pulled a long, thin blade from behind him. The light of the streetlamp reflected off of it.

"I also don't want to hurt you, Father, but I must take you home with me. We do not wish to lose you."

He made a move toward Thomas. "I will not give you pain, only a quick death, if you will allow it."

"ON A COLD DAY IN HELL, MY SON! Not as a steer but only as the bull in the ring will I accept that kind of end." Thomas pulled his sash from his cassock, twisted the ends around the fists of both his hands, and positioned himself into a fighter's stance.

"Father, you know not of what you speak. I'm trying to help you remember. *I* am not the villain. It must be this way, or all will be confused again." The man moved to the left and right, trying to thrust cleanly at Thomas.

Thomas evaded him, continuing to stand his ground firmly. "Who are you? Who sent you here?"

"I am Buer, and I come from a place where there is only light and happiness. I will take you there with me this night." The man lunged at Thomas' chest.

Thomas parried and struck him on his face, driving him against the rail above the canal. "Buer was a Demon, if my theology does not fail me!" A well-placed kick to the knee dropped the man to the ground in pain. Another left-hand blow to the side of the man's head, driven with all Thomas' strength, sent the knife from his hand. It clattered on the cobbles and dropped into the canal.

"A false claim. An angel who rebelled and yet found grace." The man pulled himself up and straightened himself as he stepped back.

"Demon or angel, it does not matter now." Thomas tied his sash back around his waist and resumed his fighter's stance. "If you wish not to be hurt again, leave now with God's blessings and mine. I shall forgive your stupidity, but not if you stay and make me hurt you."

"Father, I took the form of a man as so not to stand out, but…"

Suddenly from nowhere came a bright, almost cloudlike, light from the darkness. It grabbed the man and pulled him over the rail and into the canal. Thomas rushed to the edge and looked down. There was no sign of anything in the water but a ripple where something was sinking. He half expected to see something rise. But nothing did. Thomas rubbed his fist, which was beginning to hurt, and let out a sigh. *Am I going mad? Have I lost my hold on sanity?* He began to walk back to the villa. Thomas felt he should report this incident, but what was he to say? He felt exhausted now and needed to sleep. Tomorrow, he would try to make sense of it all. Right now, the adrenaline was pumping too quickly.

Chapter 9

All Saints College sat just outside Faneuil Hall in downtown Boston. Though one of the oldest colleges in the United States, the college had experienced a marked decline in enrollment over the past two decades, primarily due to the *Boston Globe's* Pulitzer Prize-winning coverage on the Catholic Church's sex abuse scandal. "There is little doubt the Church has brought a lot of this trouble on itself," Father Albert Kennedy once commented to David Wright. Also, working against favorable enrollment numbers was the new wave of Catholics. They were becoming more practical than devout, more concerned about lifestyle than final judgment. Still, All Saints held on, teaching young men to become ordained priests within the fifteen-hundred-year-old organization, which, according to David, was an absolute master of using fear to control the masses.

David had never been able to reconcile Father Kennedy's relationship with the institution of a single religion since his depth and breadth of knowledge of various religions was so considerable. His familiarity with ancient religions, their practices, and beliefs bordered on encyclopedic. His ability to critically compare ideological systems was a spectacle to behold. Among the faithful, many found his views out of sync with their Catholic education and beliefs. Kennedy cared little about public opinion. In 2017, he made Boston headlines when *The Herald* quoted him declaring he was "quite unsure any of the precepts of divine grace or inheritance of reward following a faithful life held any sway in the hereafter." Most people who read the article would never have known Kennedy never actually believed that. He was just pissed the paper had called him, fishing for quotes for a Halloween article on demonic possessions to push paper sales without doing any actual research on the subject. In retrospect, Kennedy probably helped them sell more papers while simultaneously causing quite the situation for himself in the diocese. In David Wright's opinion, he was a contradiction at best and one of the most enjoyable men he ever had the pleasure of knowing.

Father Graham was in his office when David arrived at his doorway. He was shuffling papers and his white hair stuck up in riotous clumps. A pure and straightforward manager with a Roman collar, his world was made up of facts, figures, debits, and credits. How to keep the lights on in the building was as important to him as his morning Vespers.

"Ah, David, there you are. Come in, and please sit." He motioned to a chair across from him. "This is a sticky business, as you can imagine. I have compiled a record of the last week or so of Father Kennedy's activities and actions. Also, everything we know about his death. There is a copy in this file of the police report, which doesn't say much except Albert M. Kennedy, Catholic Priest assigned to All Saint's College killed himself by self-inflicted gunshot to the head." He handed David the file. It was clear he just wanted this to go away to get back to his normal processing of information and handling of the school. He had known Kennedy for ten years, yet there was not one word of regret or sadness, which David found very strange. David simply nodded.

"Here is where Kennedy is right now: Boston Coroner's Office. They did the autopsy early this morning, and there was nothing remarkable about it except the extent of premature aging Kennedy's body demonstrated." David was taken back by the attitude being displayed by Father Graham toward Father Kennedy. No longer did he refer to him as 'Father.' Clearly, the act of suicide justified the action in Graham's mind. He would deal with the matter as though Kennedy was not part of the Church, nor deserving of any recognition for his years of devoted service, or the personal burdens he had encountered in discharging his duties. David resisted the childish urge to punch him in his sanctimonious mouth. The probability was high he would never see this man again, though, so why bother.

"I made arrangements for you at the Oasis Hotel near the public buildings since there is little chance of getting into the office of the coroner this late in the afternoon. As such, this matter will have to be addressed in the morning. Also, as I told you, the files go to Rome. However, before you leave our school today, I would like you to look through his office and identify anything of a personal nature you would like to keep. The rest of his belongings will be sent to a thrift shop we operate on behalf of the school. Pile the books you wish to keep in the center of his office, and I will have an acolyte box them up and send them off to you." He paused and looked down at his desk. "I think that is all, David. Again, thank you for coming down so quickly. You take a great burden off the Church and me. As I said earlier, our hands are very much tied in this matter." He stood up, signaling to David he was being dismissed. *Case closed. What was next in the in-basket?* David thought.

David shook Graham's hand reluctantly and then asked if someone could show him to Albert's office. Graham gestured to the door and told him someone would be waiting outside to assist him. The whole meeting lasted ten minutes or less; no condolences, less concern about why this happened, and a general feeling of gladness this incident was no longer his problem. Kennedy had shared with David once Father Graham despised Kennedy's work, and more so, because it was connected to the school. Graham believed exorcism was something that should have been left in the Middle Ages and forgotten. Not so in Rome's view. *They only had six confirmed exorcists east of the Mississippi and enough calls from other parishes to warrant six more. Now they only had five, and that burden would show itself very soon,* David surmised.

"Oh, one other thing, David," Father Graham called to him just as he stepped out of his office. "There was a young lady that came by earlier enquiring about Kennedy."

"Oh?" David responded.

"Yes. A lovely woman, but somewhat strange with an Italian accent.

"Did she say why she was looking for him?"

"No, but she also didn't appear terribly surprised when I informed her that Albert had 'passed away'." Graham made the air quotes motion with his fingers, suggesting to David Graham felt a level of compunction for having covered up Albert's actual cause of death.

"How were things left?"

"She asked who would be handling his affairs and enquired into whether I could provide her with the individual's contact information." Graham just stared at David for a moment as if he had concluded the discussion.

"And did you?"

"Heaven's no, David!" Graham sounded insulted by the question. I had absolutely no idea who she was, and she certainly wasn't volunteering any information. For all I knew, she could have been one of the crazies who periodically darkened the doorsteps here looking for Kennedy."

"Did you get her name?"

"I most certainly did not. I did not want to provide her any expectation that someone may be 'following up' with her." For the second time, Graham used his fingers to make air quotes.

"Good to know, I guess," David said, now sounding irritated himself. *Why would he bother telling me this if all he did was dismiss her on her way without getting any information?* The entire exchange made David realize how much he disliked Graham. David turned and left the office.

As he walked down the hallway, David reflected on the words he had written in his first book to describe the subject of exorcism. *Exorcism in the Roman Catholic Church is a delicate subject. Fighting evil in general and promising paradise for a good life is the bread and butter of the Church. However, fighting evil is about sin and atonement; it is not about fighting actual evil in the form of invisible beings that can possess and wreck a life. Evil is a tool the Church needs to keep the whole mechanism running and granting political and social power to a small and exclusive group of men in Rome. Without evil, there is little reason for the existence of the Church. For men like Father Albert Kennedy though, who went through the most brutal training program to become certified to fight real evil, an entirely different opinion existed on the subject.*

"The Church has built a remarkable defense wall," Kennedy had told him. "Extremely difficult for anyone to scale to obtain help in real matters of possession. The folks seeking help must overcome six to eight hurdles placed in their path, and only after all the requirements have been met, will the Church reluctantly send out one of their own with the hope it can be handled with as little publicity as possible."

At the end of the hallway, David arrived at the desk of Father Graham's office assistant, Mrs. Jordan, who had several documents in need of David's signature. They included a hold harmless agreement and consent to take possession of church property, i.e., Father Kennedy's remains, which caught David as a bizarre way of classifying someone. Lastly, there was a request for him to submit a final report, as brief and straightforward as possible, regarding his actions to these requirements.

David signed all the documents, and Mrs. Jordan handed him a large envelope in which she placed copies for his records. She then gave him another smaller envelope containing three hundred dollars. David held it out, "What is this about?"

Mrs. Jordan replied flatly, "It is to cover your expenses in handling this matter." David handed the envelope back to her, smiled politely, and declined to accept. She then proceeded to call out to a pale, skinny, red-haired young man sitting on a bench in robes and reading what appeared to be a psalmist or brevet. "Jimmy, please take Dr. Wright to Father Kennedy's office." The young man nodded, got up, and started to walk down the hallway with David following close behind.

When they arrived on the third floor, which looked more like a garret than a floor, Jimmy opened a door and stood back, allowing David to enter first. Jimmy then followed and sat down on one of the chairs, folding his hands in his lap.

David speculated Albert's office was unlike any of the other priests at All Saints College. It was an awkward mixture of a science workshop, archival library, and indoor swap meet. Lit by two tubular florescent lights, the office contained a large wooden desk buried beneath piles of books, folders, and notepads. There was also a certain amount of electronic equipment, including a desktop computer, two laptops, a combination scanner copier, and several different DSLR cameras. Two leather chairs faced the desk and were separated by a wooden table. The perimeter of the office was lined with several bookshelves filled with books on world religions, modern and ancient, and two entire shelves of tomes on demonology and demon sightings. The shelves included books dating back to the seventeenth- and eighteenth-century writings, opposing the Church's stance on evil and embraced Satan as Master. *Books that four hundred years ago would have gotten you burned at the stake.*

"Did you know him well?" the acolyte asked.

"Yes, I did. Very well. Father Kennedy was a close and dear friend." David answered while running his hands across the books. "Did you?"

"Yes, I have worked with Father Kennedy for the last two years. I planned to follow in his path until yesterday." It was the first time David noticed his sad eyes. He clearly had been crying.

"Not a good choice of mentors if you wish to move up the food chain in this organization." David spotted two books he had never noticed before. Old, some mold at the edges, but unique in their nature and engaging in their content.

"I never cared about that. He had a knowledge few others possessed and could do things that every priest should be able to do but can't." An interesting statement from someone so young.

"Yes, he did." David studied the young man. "Is it Jimmy, or do you prefer James?"

"James is my preference, but it is hard to get other people, especially my elders, to acknowledge that. Most still see me as a young student. Still innocent to the ways of the world." The sarcasm was heavy in his voice.

97

"And you are not?" David decided to follow the conversation path down the road to see if James could enlighten him as to what had occurred here.

"One does not go through two exorcisms and remain innocent to anything, doctor." The comment hit David powerfully. He was unaware Father Kennedy had taken on an assistant. He certainly made no mention of it to him. On three occasions, David had been with him, more out of morbid curiosity than anything related to religion. Yet, Kennedy had roped him into helping with prayers David did not believe in.

"I read the reports he wrote about your involvement and was most interested in why he would choose a non-believer, to assist him in truly the most dangerous rituals within the Church. I mean, you are not Catholic, and I do not believe you are a Christian either. I mean no disrespect."

David noted the strength of character within this young man and sensed his degree of loss. He imagined James could do much better in the world by going through a science program at a good school and perhaps, head off to graduate studies. *A mind is a terrible thing to waste, especially when it's spent on superstition and trivial aspects of some bygone meaning.*

"Father Kennedy did not see his work as religious; I don't know if you know that or not. He saw the tools he used as religious, but that was only due to the prevailing course in the Western World. I viewed him more as a shaman or witch doctor, dealing with evil. He could have been using a clamshell and a string of beads from the South Pacific, as far as I could tell. He fought evil with goodness, not faith." David paused. He had never put it into words before, and he realized that it was the actual reason he had worked with him. *He was just as much of a therapist as me.*

"I do see it as religious, and that is what attracted me to the study and my desire to be like Father Kennedy. My academic major is in clinical psychology, and I am extremely interested in learning the distinction between purely psychological troubles and those things I have witnessed with my own eyes that are not from within our minds." James was articulate and careful in his choice of words. "Would you mind answering a question for me, Dr. Wright?"

David identified a very mature quality within James not obvious on his surface. "If I am able," David replied.

"Do you believe in all of this?" James motioned his hands in a wide swath around the contents of the room.

David stared at James and subtly grimaced. "I believe Father Kennedy believed in demonic possession. I believed in Father Kennedy. And I believe he genuinely helped these people through an affliction of the worst sort." James dropped his gaze from David and looked down at the floor, seeming disheartened by David's response.

"Why do you think he did *this*?" David stood looking out the small window and across the courtyard of the college.

"They were getting too close to him," James answered while lifting the cushion of the other chair. He pulled out a small package of brown wrapping paper bound in tape and twine. "This is for you. He told me you would come and when you did, I was to hand you this personally, or if not, I was to take it to you at your home."

"What is this?" David turned it over in his hand. "Feels like a book."

"Probably the most dangerous book in existence. Father Kennedy told me about it and equally, was unprepared to let me read it just yet. He wanted you to have it. There is a letter inside you are not to read until you get home."

"He told you all of this? When?" David asked while taking the package from him.

"A week ago. I suspected something would happen, but I did not foresee Father Kennedy killing himself. This past month he was tormented almost every night to the point of sleeping exclusively during the day. On a few occasions, he had asked if I would sit with him and 'stand watch' so he could get a few hours of sleep."

"What frightened him so badly, James?" He had utterly stirred David's curiosity by now.

"A demon. The one from his last case. Father had driven it so relentlessly to leave the young girl it had been infecting, it screamed to him he would be next. From that day forward, everything was different. The demon knew his name, and it hunted him. At night, I would find Father in the small chapel downstairs, praying and meditating. It was the only place he could go where he wasn't being tormented." James told the story, like any story, plain and clear, yet its implications were dreadful.

"Did you ever see or hear anything that would lead you to believe, perhaps, Father Kennedy had slipped into his delusion?" David knew working in this particular field had some significant drawbacks compared to living what many would consider a 'normal' life.

"Not directly, but I saw the wounds he endured. Streaks of scratches running down his back, bruising on his legs, arms, and back. A week ago, he put that package together, and he told me he was terrified as to what would happen next. I attempted to calm him, but I found I could say nothing that would soothe him. He was a man convinced and, on a mission, to clean everything up before the end. Father Kennedy had me burn several files he did not want Rome to acquire. Such a shame; so many secrets died with him." James stood up from the chair. "Which of the books would you like sent to you?"

"Are there any you would like?" David asked.

"Yes, all of them, truth be known. But I could not take them nor keep them here. Father Graham would undoubtedly find out, and I would be in the untenable position of explaining myself, my interests, and my concerns with them. He is passionately opposed to me continuing down this path I am on." James ran his hands over the volumes on the shelves and murmured, "So much knowledge."

"Send them all up to me—every one of them. I will keep them for you until you are ready to collect them. I may read one or two in the meantime." David attempted a smile. "But consider them yours."

"Thank you, Dr. Wright. I truly appreciate the gesture." James nodded, and began to leave, and then suddenly stopped. "Her name was Dr. Pellegrini," he said, looking down at something he now held in his hand.

"What?" David asked, giving James a questioning look.

"The woman Father Graham mentioned who was here earlier and looking for Father Kennedy. She asked me to give you this." James handed David the business card he had been holding.

David looked down at the card. *Lorenza Pellegrini, PhD. Consultant, Antiquarian Books.* The card listed offices in Rome, Florence, and Venice along with several phone numbers. "I thought Father Graham said he dismissed her without any exchange of information?"

"He did," James replied. "But I stopped her while she was leaving to enquire as to why she was looking for Father Kennedy."

"Oh?" David said, now appearing very interested.

"She said she was looking for a very old and unique book she believed Father had in his custody."

David looked around the room and smirked. "I wonder whatever could have given a person such an idea?"

"I brought her up here," James said.

"You did?"

Now looking a little embarrassed, James said, "Yes."

"And did she find the book she was referring to?"

"No. She went through each of the shelves, one by one, carefully inspecting them. Even placing her hand behind the books to see if anything may have been hidden, out of the line of sight. But she didn't come across the one she was looking for."

"So, Father Kennedy didn't have the one she was referring to?" David queried.

"I believe he did," James replied, now staring at David. "And I believe it is within the package you now hold in your hands." James bowed his head slightly, indicating he was leaving, and walked out of the office.

As David stood there in the middle of the small office that had been Albert's headquarters for so long, he studied his surroundings. For a man who had done great and dangerous work, he had little in the way of earthly joys to accompany such deeds. David thought about Father Graham's dismissal of all of this and was overcome with an overwhelming feeling of loss and pure sadness for his friend. He reflected on the entirety of the situation, the package he held in his hand and the odd conversation James had relayed about this mystery woman. *Probably the most dangerous book in existence.*

Chapter 10

Thomas was lying in the darkness of his room. What had happened earlier seemed inexplicable. Secretly, he had always snickered at those who spoke of *evil* being real. He accepted the concept, but only in terms of discerning human shortcomings. As far as tangible evil in human form, Thomas had relegated that to the rest of the myths surrounding religion. Accepting the sacraments as a way of life was a good measure to ensure a decent existence. The rest of the theology concerning the struggle between good and evil was quaint to him—better left to fiction writers and movie companies. But what he had witnessed tonight forced him to question whether there was a supernatural side to life—a side he had been too ignorant or egotistical to accept. The bones he felt break under his fist earlier were those of a man. But whatever came from the darkness and took that man into the canal's waterway was not of this world.

Sweat covered his body, and he stared wide-eyed toward the ceiling, which he could not see in the darkness. His world was of scholar's facts; it was not built around conflicts between forces he did not understand. Half a hundred thoughts raced through the electrochemical system of his brain, and none of them made any sense at all. *Should I pick up my things and leave in the middle of the night? Should I find a church to go pray within? Could I just take his notes and return home to finish the book, hoping to let time diminish the uncomfortable memories? Does the book even matter at this point? Do I?* Thomas felt palpable isolation. Fear coursed through his entire being, and he found himself starting to tremble.

It came first as a sensation. A kind of primordial knowledge something or someone else was in the room with him. Thomas didn't turn his head to look around, but lay there silently waiting...for what, he could not say. *Did the deranged man escape the canal? Did this obvious psychotic follow me here somehow, and is he now standing in the doorway? What if he's gripping his knife again and still intent on taking my life?* Thomas could feel a presence moving about silently and watching him. He considered yelling out. But what good would that do? He could try to get out from under the covers, but that would take time he did not have. Closing his eyes very tightly, Thomas tried to pray, but his mind went blank. Then he felt breath on his face; whoever was there in the room with him was now leaning in close and smelling him. Thomas's heart felt as if it was about to stop. Fear—pure fear—engulfed him. He tightened his body as if that would help, but it was just a physical response to the presence of something so close. One of his most secret fears exploded within his mind. Now he would know the ultimate truth. *Is there something after this life we pretend to know about and teach our parishioners? Or is there just the dark black nothingness of oblivion that will allow us no knowledge of life's greatest mystery?*

Thomas suddenly felt a heaviness through the covers as something was holding his hand down. It was an actual manifestation. This was not a dream or a hysterical reaction on his part.

He tried again to find a prayer in his head...the one used at the point when someone was dying. But all he found was fear. A strange numbness had started to set in. *Is this the precursor to death? How could this be? I still have so many things I want to do, places to see, and...my book. I want to finish my book.* It had taken years out of his life, and he had spent so much time on it. It was the one point of light in Thomas's world providing him a sense of meaning as to what he was doing on this earth.

He felt something soft, brush against his face. It was like a soft hairbrush just stroking his cheek. Thomas could feel a teardrop escape from the corner of his eye and roll slowly down his cheek. Another soon followed it.

The heaviness moved from his arm to his chest. Thomas would die without seeing what it was that was about to kill him. He needed to open his eyes. He owed that much to himself.

Thomas forced his eyes open and saw the shadow standing over him.

His mouth opened to form a scream, but nothing came out. Then the specter moved forward and thrust its face into his. It licked the tear from his cheek and ran a rough tongue around his neck. Thomas grabbed for some matches on the sideboard next to the bed and lit one. He saw Aza standing over him, pushing his face into Thomas's and purring loudly. Thomas felt his body collapse from fatigue and dropped the match to the floor, where it immediately went out.

"My God, Aza...you scared me!" Thomas pulled the covers back and swung out into a sitting position to light another match for the candle. Thomas held Aza's head in both of his hands and placed his forehead against his. Aza's purr intensified, and Thomas patted his side. Thomas's bowels were like hot liquid, and he needed to use the lavatory right away. Thomas got up and went into it, taking the candle with him.

Aza followed him and curled up on the bathroom floor. He lay there watching him. Thomas tried to slow down his breathing. He also took a moment to get his heartbeat lowered once again. Finally, he started to cry. Not softly, but with all his emotions flooding to the surface. There was no stopping them. He hung over the sink, where he got sick and felt everything run out of him simultaneously.

Finally, he had regained some control. Thomas walked back into the bedroom with Aza by his side, and pulled a blanket from the bed, wrapping it tightly around him. He lay on the floor next to the leopard, getting as close as he could, and draped an arm over Aza's chest. Between exhaustion and the feeling of protection this creature offered him, Thomas dropped into a very deep and dreamless sleep.

Chapter 11

The Boston Morgue is located at 720 Albany Street, just across from Boston Medical and about two miles south of All Saints College. The morgue houses the Office of the Massachusetts Chief Medical Examiner (OCME). As one of the largest medical examiner systems in the United States, with a jurisdiction serving 6.8 million people, the OCME is responsible for determining the cause and manner of deaths that are not of obvious natural causes. Approximately 15,000 deaths are reported to the OCME on an annual basis. Just two days prior, Father Albert Kennedy's had been registered amongst them.

David presented his paperwork at the front desk of the office. The man at the counter looked through it and filled out another form carefully. The man didn't say much, giving off the impression this was all routine. He glanced at the custodian papers the Church had given David to dispose of his friend's body. He had seen those before as well. When everything was done paperwork-wise, he asked David which funeral home he wanted to use. David shared with the man the one he had selected the night before while in his hotel room. He had spoken to someone on duty, to firm up rates and the method of transport. The home evidently would handle everything, from picking up the body to dealing with the cremation. David had decided if that is what Albert wanted, then that was what he would have. They had billed his credit card and told him to call in the morning after he was finished at the OCME.

David asked to see Father Kennedy, to which the attendant begrudgingly agreed. Generally, those requests were denied as the part of the facility holding the cadavers, wasn't designed for public visitors. The morgue would set up private viewings if one requested such in advance, but David hadn't, and so he requested the viewing in the large room housing the other corpses. He informed the man he was a medical professional, and it wouldn't bother him. *I just wanted to pay my last respects.* The man requested David spend no more than five minutes in the room, then check in with him before leaving. David had nodded his agreement.

David was taken into a large room where Father Kennedy's body had been placed in the middle. He pulled the sheet back carefully from Kennedy's face, not sure what to expect. *Bullet wounds were always messy.* David looked on in surprise. Kennedy used a small-caliber weapon he placed in his mouth, and the bullet had never exited the brain vault. David noticed Kennedy looked almost peaceful, laying there as if he was just asleep. It was the first time David noticed just how cold the room was. It seemed much colder than he had remembered from the previous times he had been in the room over the years while practicing in Boston. David pulled up the collar on his jacket.

David looked down at the wrinkled and leathery face. He thought it looked like a road map of small etched lines and deep crevasses, which gave his face character. He had deep dark splashes below his eyes, clearly the result of trauma from the wound. David picked up one of his hands and held it to his chest for a moment. He felt the gentleness of it as well as the coldness, and then laid it back down next to his body and ran his hand through his gray and silver hair. Kennedy appeared to be a man of seventy-five, and David presumed was the reason why no one bothered to do a complete autopsy on him. There was no 'Y' cut on his chest where bodies are generally cut open, and everything pulled out to be looked at and examined under a microscope. Indifference to death was a hallmark of this place. David supposed that trait was necessary to survive in a job like this.

Find the cause of death, write it down, move on to the next person. It was a gunshot wound to the mouth and into the brain. Period.

David rubbed his hands through his hair and felt the texture, noticing how his hair formed a spiral at the crown. Father Albert Kennedy had turned fifty-six years old last September. His face, hair, and body all appeared twenty years older than that, which David suspected resulted from the work he had done. *Every exorcism takes its toll in years and health*. David remembered Kennedy saying so once, which he ended up quoting in his book. *A fact that is not advertised very much. At best, he probably had one more exorcism left in him*, David thought, simply based on how he looked. *Fight whatever demons people are facing, and you pay the price.* He had always talked about that fact with David and his premature aging. Kennedy hated it, and David didn't understand it. But evidently, it went with the territory.

"Why didn't you call me first?" David growled to the man on the table. For the first time during all of this, David began to cry.

The door opened, and the attendant came in telling him his time was up and he had to leave. David wiped his eyes with his fingers and nodded at the attendant. He touched Albert one last time, pulled the cover back over his face, and walked out.

***

114

The Liberty Hotel is one of the most iconic buildings nestled in the Beacon Hill neighborhood, situated just north of Boston Common. Since 1851, it has been a place most people have avoided spending a night in, as it was formerly the Charles Street Jail. The mid-19th century granite-style building was a collaboration between architect Gridley James Fox Bryant, one of Boston's most talented architects of the time, and the Reverend, Louis Dwight, a Yale-educated penologist and staunch advocate for prison reform. After a long-distinguished and storied history, in 1990, the inmates of the Charles Street Jail were moved for the final time, and the building's metamorphosis began. Now, sitting in a chair in one of the rooms within the hotel, Lorenza Pellegrini stared down at her laptop. *Let us find out just who you are, Dr. David Wright.*

Chapter 12

It was late in the morning when Thomas finally awoke. He was back in his bed and lying there in a peaceful state. It seemed as if the night terrors afflicting him had given way to the morning sun, and everything seemed different. He checked his phone for messages and noticed a text from Lorenza asking him to stay a few more days, as she was eager to hear about what he had discovered in his research upon her return. She also mentioned the Master of the house had been tied up longer than expected but wanted to host a dinner in a few days she didn't want him to miss. Thomas decided a few more days would be welcomed in finalizing some items and allowing him to get some more photographs. Thomas noted he felt composed and surprisingly full of energy. *I do believe a morning run is in my future.*

As Thomas headed out the door of the villa, he ran north along the canal. As he ran, his eyes took in his surroundings, while his mind drifted on the history of this city and how it was described by Bruno and others in their writings.

The influence of a thousand cultures had left its mark within the confines of this city. The great caravans of the medieval period started in China along a massive circuit of routes which came to be known as the Silk Road. The roads ran between small and large areas, branching out and converging, so the world's wares could be traded, bought, and sold. Western merchants would bring various strange and unique goods back, via a long line of camels to the ports on the Mediterranean. Venice's merchants would trade in porcelain, silk, spices, and a thousand other things the Europeans had never seen before. All came through this one city making its living on the commerce of the world.

The greatest map makers of the medieval world plied their abilities here, creating the charts that showed what lay beyond the horizons. These monks who spent years drawing a single map were considered the 'Masters of Geography,' next only to Ptolemy of Alexandria. A map that would lead one from Venice to Samarqand was worth a hundred thousand gold ducats—a king's ransom and then some. Thus, they were guarded by the Church, and only the greatest of households could afford such maps. The maps were reasonably reliable and would sometimes have only a slight imperfection. The Church made maps, and the merchants made money. The merchants were only too happy to give willingly to the Church to keep the Church from trying to share in the profit of exploiting the East of its treasures.

With commerce, comes some strange ideas and customs, and in this respect, the East had an influence in Venice that reached far deeper than anyone expected or wanted. The mysteries of Eastern religions and sects spread to even the most devout families. Books passed through this city that came from Constantinople and were then reprinted in Venice to travel the hidden highways of Europe. These tomes would end up in the hands of those who had the money and the understanding that there were greater mysteries in the world than those of which the clerics spoke. Sufism, Zoroastrianism, Hinduism, and the black arts of magic were hidden behind secret panels and tucked away in the back of bookshops. These books were only to be sold to those known to the proprietor on a personal level, and it was understood that the possession of them, could equate to a death sentence from the Church.

Yet, among the elite, this knowledge flourished, and was passed from house to house by those who wanted to know what was out there in the world. A single book might be worth all a man could make in his entire lifetime. Those who had several or *hundreds, were considered the billionaires of their time. Clerics were lured from the Church to hide in upstairs rooms for years to translate a single text. For that service, one would receive a life of luxury beyond all comparison. The languages of Arabia, Greece, and Asia become a bargaining chip in the game of life and death in this city. Those who could translate, were both wanted and hunted by the two sides of the game of knowledge.*

All of those ideas and thoughts passed through Thomas before he stopped to look into a window of a bookbinder on Spadaria San Mateo, between the Piazza St. Marco and Ponte di Rialto Bridge. As he began running again, he turned north and headed for St. Maria Formosa. Between the two points, was the Church of St. John the Baptist, the small church he visited the day before and received the gift of the crucifix from Father Novelli. It was nearly noon, and the streets before him were quiet when he stopped running. He walked to the door of the church and gave it a gentle push. The door yielded and opened for him. As he walked into the darkened interior, Thomas could smell incense burning and see candles flickering from the offering table next to a side altar.

He stood there for a moment, letting his eyes adjust to the darkness and admiring the ancient architecture of the church. Within a few moments, the high ceiling, the vaulted dome, and the nave came into focus for him, and he began to study the plaques on the wall. This church had been founded in the 1400s and still served its parishioners today.

He noticed a priest working up at the altar, busying himself with something. Thomas walked up to the railing to genuflect and bow his head, and then made the sign of the cross over his chest before passing through the gate leading up to the altar.

When the priest caught notice of Thomas, he was visibly alarmed and held up his hands gesturing to Thomas he should not be there.

"Good morning, Father. I am Father Morelli," Thomas said.

"I am sorry, Father. I did not know. I thought you were a tourist." He spoke rather quickly.

"I wish to see Father Novelli if he is available," Thomas stated.

"Of course. Please follow me." The priest led Thomas to a side altar next to the main altar. He made the sign of the Cross over his chest and then motioned to the floor.

Thomas looked down at the area of flooring indicated by the priest and saw a grave marker. Thomas read it softly to himself: "Father B. Novelli, 1528–1605." Thomas glanced up at the priest, and Thomas could see he was staring back at him. Conscious of Thomas's uneasiness, he asked Thomas if everything was alright. Thomas nodded his head but wasn't quite sure. The priest then took his leave and walked out of the church. Thomas knelt there for a few moments looking at the stone, and thought, *This can't be happening!*

Chapter 13

Along one of the small side streets, Thomas found a bench to consider all that was happening to him. As he sat there thinking with his eyes closed, he could feel a warm afternoon breeze lazily moving up from the sea through the twists and turns of the canal's waterway. His mind replayed the past few days. The books of Bruno that shouldn't exist. The stranger in the mask. The man in the church. The creature taking his would-be assailant from the bridge. *Now...Novelli?*

When he opened his eyes, Thomas almost leapt from the bench. Sitting next to him was an old man in a flat black hat, holding a book in his hands. His rather lengthy white hair matched his beard, which hung down long enough to rest on his chest. His black outercoat only partially hid the shoulder shawl he was wearing underneath.

"The greatest difficulty in life is holding two opposing thoughts in your mind at the same time and trying to resolve both to satisfaction." He was watching the far side of the canal, and his eyes never deviated from one point.

"I was enjoying the breeze," Thomas said.

"If you say so. But in all the years I have sat up there above this bench..." He pointed to the building above without losing sight of whatever he was looking at across the canal. "...I have not seen many people caught between two worlds as you are, Father." He turned and looked at Thomas for the first time. His leathery face was hardened by wrinkles. The corner of his beard around his mouth was stained from tea. But it was his eyes Thomas noticed most: They were deep brown and still held life as a mystery; somehow, they did not seem to belong in that face.

"How did you know?" Thomas asked him quietly.

"That you were a priest? Simple. I looked down at you. "I am Rabbi Isaac." I was born seventy-two years ago in the apartment just above us."

Thomas looked at the man but didn't quite know what to say. "I am not sure what you mean, Isaac. You spoke of two worlds, and that I am seeing it now. There have been some strange things happening to

124

me of late...but nothing randomness cannot explain." This was a lie. Thomas could not explain any of it, but he felt uncomfortable with that answer.

"Father Thomas, I am a Kabbalist. I have spent my life learning the ways of the secrets of mysticism. I have never concerned myself with the debate within my community about when the works of DeLeon came into existence. Yet, I have studied the *Zohar* for fifty years. Every word of it and every sentence of it. And in doing so, I have passed through many stages of advancement required to be a master of some degree. There are one hundred and twenty degrees to Mastership within the world of the Kabbalah, and when you have mastered those, I am sure the next level of existence will hand you many more. In what I have learned, I can see those things others may not...and hear those things that are silent to many. A battle is raging here in Venice right now. Forces of darkness and light are struggling together to gain ground. You, for some reason, have been selected to be part of all of this. I am not sure why. But I can tell you are particularly important in this struggle." Isaac sat back and folded his hands over the book now on his lap.

A year ago—no, two weeks ago—Thomas would have laughed at the quaintness of his words. But right now, Thomas was not at all amused. Thomas looked carefully at him as the man nodded.

"You know something is not right. Do you not?" Isaac looked past Thomas across the canal. "He was watching you, Thomas."

125

"Pardon?" Thomas asked. "Who's watching me, Isaac? What do you mean?"

"He is gone now. But earlier, an angel stood on the far shore watching you with great concern in his eyes."

"An angel?" Thomas asked incredulously.

"Indeed." Isaac nodded. "The sun has not yet set...so you are still safe for an hour or so, but you should leave with all haste and return to wherever it is you find safety. Please, do not hesitate. May the blessings stay with you through your night of obscureness." Isaac reached over and took Thomas's hand to kiss it gently. "Go now, Father Thomas. My prayers are with you."

Thomas got up and leaned down next to the old man. He touched his head gently with the palm of his hand. "May God bless you and protect you." Thomas turned and left without another word.

Chapter 14

Back at his home, David was now sitting at his desk, studying the package from Kennedy. He carefully cut the manila hemp that was bound and sealed around the brown wrapping paper. There was another layer inside the outer one. Also enclosed, was an envelope that said, *Read First*. David ripped it open and took out a couple of sheets of cheap copier paper. In Albert's fine and delicate script, he had written a letter to him. Each letter of every word was perfectly formed, and his handwriting so precise, it looked almost typewritten. David studied both pieces of paper before beginning to read. It was not a letter of great length, but based on David's quick scan, it was quite substantial.

Dear David,

I am sorry I had to pull you into this quagmire, but I had no place else to turn. My days are numbered now, I know. I can no longer fight the forces trying to destroy me and my work. You may think your involvement with me was some unique opportunity you were given to witness things and events no human should ever see. But it was not. Your books were a sidelight to what was really happening. It was just that I could never bring myself to face you and tell you the truth.

When I was in the seminary, I was selected to spend three years in Rome at the Vatican, at the request of an elderly Cardinal, Matteo Brambilla. Brambilla was quite a fascinating individual, and his history with the Vatican was even more intriguing. You see, Brambilla had access to everything within the Holy See. No part or place was restricted to him, and he had used that power to gain access to some of the most hidden and arcane places deep underground, in the Vatican catacombs, where there is not even electricity by which to see.

During one such expedition, Brambilla stumbled upon a book repository of sorts. Skin-wrapped tomes of books dating back hundreds of years, and a few, dating back much further. Some were sealed in lead

128

*boxes and then placed inside cedar, much
like the coffins of the Popes. Hidden among
them, he found the book you now hold in
your hands. It is a combination of many
things, as ancient texts tend to be. It is
written on human skin; the ink has traces
of human blood within it. I know this, for I
have had some of it tested independently.
The tiny parts I removed and had tested
still carried DNA markers within them.
That is a horror story all on its own. No two
pages are from the same person, that much
is clear, and there are two hundred and
forty-two pages in total. The book is
written in ancient Sumerian cuneiform. I
speculated it was because of this book, the
Arcadians used the same language. At
some point, most of the book was
translated so that the text can be read in
Latin. Each page of this book has a sheet of
foolscap octavo written on both sides that
translate each page. Keep the pages in
order and within the pages that you took
them from. If you get one translated page
out of place, the consequences would be
shattering.*

*The book was written over four
thousand years ago by a Sumerian priest
named Barkar. Barkar had been visited
one night by a traveler, an individual
named Varritain, who told him the story of
the shedim. From what can be learned, the
shedim were divine beings formed even
before the angels. At some point, Eryther,
the leader of the shedim, led a revolt in*

129

heaven; the reason is unclear. In response to this, Elohim utilized the angels, led by Lucifer, and fought a great battle to force the shedim into captivity in another 'place.' The war was horrid, cruel, brutal, and in the end, tens of millions of angels had perished. Lucifer was instrumental in confining Eryther and the shedim behind the Crystal Sphere, the barrier between our universe and this other place—a prison. This prison existed outside of this space and this time. Eryther pledged the destruction of all that was created and ever would be. When all of this happened, time as we know it had just begun its forward movement. Varritain was given the task of watching for any single entity that somehow escaped and came back into this plane of existence; many were already here. They feed on the innocent so they may remain immortal. However, their primary objective is to open the sphere and release Eryther.

Varritain told Barkar long ago, he, himself, had been chosen to be the gatekeeper among humans. Whenever one of the shedim would appear, he would travel with armed escorts from the high court of the Kings of Sumeria, to expel that shedim and attempt to send it back behind the sphere, but it never worked. Expelling the shedim from its human host body would only address the current situation, as it would always move on to the next, biding its time, waiting for the exact moment to reveal itself again. Sound familiar?

Varritain told Barkar he could no longer complete this task, as his body had grown tired, and he needed to find another to replace him. He had chosen the priest. He had chosen Barkar.

When Varritain provided Barkar with this information, he was dying from his last encounter with a shedim. He instructed Barkar to use the knowledge and hide the book and, as time went by, to give it to the next gatekeeper who would continue the battle.

Each Keeper did what was requested by the prior, as the book made its way from generation to generation, unseen by most, until four hundred years ago when it was discovered by members of the Inquisition, and purportedly fell into the hands of Giordano Bruno. During his arrest, the book was confiscated and turned over to the Holy Office and buried somewhere within it. It was believed lost until Brambilla uncovered it.

After reading only parts of the book that someone else had translated into Latin, Brambilla knew he did not dare give this book to his benefactor. It was far too important and dangerous. Just by keeping it, one draws to oneself the horrid, as it acts as a beacon to the shedim. You should know while this book speaks of how to contain them, it also speaks of releasing them from behind the Crystal Sphere.

You may choose to hide this book if it scares you too much. But understand, if you do, no one will be able to exile them truly. If you keep it, you shall be forced to fight. They are near; I can feel them. I shall not let them have me. Please know, David, this is all true. Faith in oneself and one's ability to face fear is all one has—blessings and love upon you, my dear friend. We shall speak again when we can.

Albert.

David sat looking at Kennedy's note for a moment. *Madness, delusions, schizophrenia, senility. Poor bastard bought into someone else's game and has thrown his whole life away. Demons and devils. Fallen angels and Guardians of Truth. All the myths and fables Joseph Campbell wrote about so clearly.* David placed the note down on his desk, stood up, walked over to the window, and looked out toward the ocean below. His mind kept repeating Kennedy's words over and over again. Why would he give this to me? *Latin! I don't even speak Latin.*

Chapter 15

David's reasonable mind was working through all the possibilities he could think of, concerning the reason for Albert's death. *Why didn't he call? He could have left and come up here, as he had in the past.* He looked at the book on his desk and flipped through it, being careful not to let any pages fall out or move from their location. It was a strange book, no doubt, but it just seemed old and well-worn. Staring at one loose page, he tried reading the Latin; it was ancient in its style, and some words were going to require an excellent cross-reference dictionary to understand entirely.

David typed in some of the sentences into his search browser to see if they could be easily translated. Some of the words had converted into English, and some appeared as unknowns. While looking intensely at his computer's screen, he heard a knocking coming from his front door. *Who could that be?*

David opened the door to find a stunning woman standing there. David immediately began making mental notes to himself as if he needed to memorialize her appearance in a patient file later. *Dark brown hair with light brown eyes wearing an emerald, green sleeveless dress. Toned physique. Age was roughly thirty-five years old and approximately 5'8 with an estimated weight of 128 pounds. 'Stop it!'* He said to himself and then smirked. *Old habits.*

"Dr. David Wright?" the woman asked with an accent he detected to be Italian.

"Yes?" David responded.

"My name is Dr. Lorenza Pellegrini, from Venice. I understand you may be handling the affairs of Father Albert Kennedy. My sincere condolences for your loss."

David recognized the name from the business card James had given him while at All Saints. He stared at her, not providing any responses, to see where this was going. "May I have a moment of your time? It is regarding Father Kennedy, and it is rather important."

David nodded and reluctantly let her in. His thoughts tumbled from a keen interest and fell into his usual cynicism about people. She had to be a lawyer, and now he would find out why Albert had killed himself. *Just my luck. She represented the mother of a child Albert had while he lived in Rome thirty years ago, and she is here to deliver the bill against any estate that might exist. The vultures always know where to look, even before the recently deceased are even in the ground.* David now felt himself on the defensive.

"Please, have a seat." David motioned toward one of the chairs. "May I offer you something? A cup of coffee, iced tea, water?"

"No, I am okay, thank you." She looked around at his beach house. "This is a remarkable place you have here. I love the view you have, high above the beach, and yet you can hear the surf outside."

"Thank you. I bought the place to get away from the world and so no one could find me. And yet, here you are." David sat down on the couch directly across from her, forcing a smile.

"My apologies for showing up on your porch unannounced, but I wasn't able to locate a phone number for you. I had dropped by All Saints looking for Father Kennedy and was surprised to hear about his unexpected passing from Father Graham. Before I left, I spoke with a very nice young man who said he couldn't provide me with much information, but that you had been called in to handle the affairs, which I found rather peculiar. He was a member of

135

the Church; why would a layperson be involved? Then the young man, Jimmy, I believe his name was, informed me Father Kennedy had taken his own life. I was quite shocked." Her words made David think of his friend, and sadness began to fill him once again. "Oddly enough, just two days prior, the Vatican had dispatched me to speak to him on some rather urgent matters." She sat back and looked at David, waiting for a reaction.

"You say the Vatican sent you?"

"They did." Lorenza withheld the fact her boss had also dispatched her on the same errand. "In the hope of retrieving an ancient book they believed was in Father Kennedy's possession."

"So, how did you find me? Especially so quickly?" David's mind was racing, and there was something about her—he wasn't sure what—that told him he needed to be very careful.

"Jimmy gave me your name after he allowed me to look through Father Kennedy's books. I was searching for the one I mentioned, but I was unable to locate it. I imagined he might have given it to you before he...before his death. From what I understand, you had joined him from time to time in his work and perhaps were also one of his good friends. On that, I can only speculate."

"That doesn't explain how you found me. I am sure James did not give you my address." *One step at a time*, David told himself. This was still too smooth for his liking.

"I did some research from my hotel room later in the day and found an article about an exorcism Father Kennedy had done with a layman involved. The article spoke about you in glowing tones. Psychoanalyst turned author, assisting a member of the Church in fighting demons." She smiled ever so slightly. "For better or worse, the internet is a virtual trove of information, and one can find out pretty much anything and everything on a person if one looks hard enough. Your information, however, wasn't too difficult to find at all. I put your name in and provided the general vicinity of where you once worked and *viola*. The fourth result down was a fan-created page that provided your address here in Portside, a picture of the front of your house, and the view from your back deck. From that, I now had a place to embark on my search in locating you."

"Gotta love the obsessive fan-stalkers." David now laughed nervously as he discovered his life was much more of an open book than he cared to acknowledge.

"I then hired a car and driver in Boston, who, by the way, is currently parked at the bottom of your driveway, and had him bring me here. I didn't fly up on a broomstick if that is what you are thinking." She laughed gently, causing David to laugh a bit harder. He had to admit, everything about her was cute.

"You know, I had you pegged as an attorney," he said.

"Well, I am sorry to disappoint you." Lorenza now smiled a very wide and lovely smile.

"Stop it! I am quite relieved." David held up his hand in jest and smiled.

Lorenza smiled, but then her face took on a more serious expression. "So, may I now ask, did he give you a book—a very *special* book?" She sat there looking intensely into his eyes.

David studied her for a few moments, trying to determine his next course of action. He decided her answer to his next question would determine how much information he would share with her.

"Tell me, Dr. Pellegrini, by any chance, do you read Latin?"

Chapter 16

David walked Lorenza over to his desk, where the book was lying open. He pointed at the page it was opened to and asked, "Any idea as to what the translation of this is?" David waited, holding his breath.

"For you are already excommunicated, praise your Lord, for he is not coming," Lorenza said and then waited a long minute, looking down at the book. David just stood there looking at her. How could she have known what the missing word was?

"Maranatha? It is not Latin," David said very quietly.

"Mara Natha. Aramaic. For praise your lord. Only used once in the New Testament and once in Didache 10:14 of the Apostolic Father's Collection."

"What does it mean?"

"It's a curse. It says by possessing this book, you are already condemned, and pray as much as you wish; your God will not come and save you from the horrors waiting inside this tome." She stood there looking at him. "It goes on to state, 'Whoever opens this book and reads from it shall have the fate of the world tied to his wills and have the world forever seeking to devour his soul'."

"Excuse me?" David blurted.

"Do you have any idea why Father Kennedy would want you to have this book?"

"Absolutely no idea. I have never even seen this book until today. He never had it with him during his exorcisms and never even spoke of it."

"David, the Vatican claimed they gave him this book in aiding him to perform exorcisms. However, based on what we just read, I highly doubt that to be true. Nonetheless, they are adamant about having this book in their possession."

"Who does? The Pope?" David enquired.

"I don't believe the interest rises that high, but a certain cardinal in the College does."

David flipped to another page in the book with an illustration depicting winged beings throwing dark creatures through what looked to be a doorway in the sky. "Any idea what this represents?"

"I have seen something like this before in the dungeons of Venice. It represents the Crystal Sphere."

David stared at Lorenza for a long time and then back down at the book. "What in the hell is a Crystal Sphere?"

"*The* Crystal Sphere," Lorenza corrected him.

"*The* Crystal Sphere." David repeated, using the same emphasis as Lorenza. "What in the hell is *The* Crystal Sphere?"

"It is said the Crystal Sphere is the access point to a place, a pocket universe if you will, that exists outside of our known four-dimensional field, or applying a more generally utilized but largely misapplied term, 'the space-time continuum.' This place was used for the Demons as a humane method of imprisoning them - to prevent further bloodshed of both angels and demons during the Erytherian Uprising."

"I'm sorry, during what?" David responded, appearing frustrated while closing his eyes and shaking his head.

"I'm very sorry, David. I know this is a lot to take in," Lorenza said softly while putting her hand on his shoulder. "Would you mind taking a walk with me? I would like to show you something."

David stared at the book and then up at Lorenza. She had a consoling smile on her face, and her brown eyes appeared incredibly warm and comforting to him at this very moment. Not answering, David gently closed the book and stood up while carrying it back to the safe. Crouching down, he placed the book inside, closed the door, and then set the lock. For a moment, he just stared at the keypad on the safe's door, contemplating what Lorenza had just shared. As he stood up, he grabbed his coat from the back of his desk chair. Placing it on, he could not help but think, *what is she possibly going to show me now?*

Once they were both outside, Lorenza turned and looked at David very seriously, staring into his green eyes for a good moment. "David?" she said. "How does one get down to the beach?"

David looked at Lorenza and could not control the laugh that sounded more like a chortle. He wasn't sure if it was a laugh of relief or surprise at her question, but he didn't care. All David knew, was he was happy for a change in conversation and felt a return to normalcy. "Follow me," he said with a big smile. "Oh, and watch your step."

The staircase leading to the beach below was about twenty feet behind David's house. It was evident that its original color was white, but time and the elements had given way to a more weathered appearance, reflecting a more greyish brown color than white. The saltwater splashed against the steps had caused some of them to rot considerably. On one step in particular, Lorenza felt her foot nearly step through the entire plank, but she managed to brace herself on the equally beach-worn rails, preventing what would have become a genuinely embarrassing event. "You ever consider replacing some of these

142

steps?" she yelled ahead to David, as she regained her balance and continued down.

"All the time," David said as he laughed and stomped his way down the remaining steps and onto the sand.

At the bottom of the descent and safely in the sand, Lorenza looked up the staircase leading back to the house and asked, "Have you ever counted how many there are?"

"253," David replied immediately, almost as if he knew she was going to ask him that question.

"And is this the only one that gets us back up there?" Lorenza asked, obviously internally debating if she wanted to make the return trip.

"No," David replied. "There is another one about three and a half miles down the beach. A really nice metal one," he said with a boyish smile.

Lorenza let out a laugh and then put her hand on David's shoulder to brace herself, while she took off her shoes one by one. Once both of her shoes were off, she smiled at David and asked, "Do you need to borrow a shoulder as well?" Sticking her right shoulder out in a lighthearted manner.

"Don't mind if I do," David replied.

After David had his bare feet in the sand, Lorenza interlocked her right arm into his left arm and pulled him in the direction of the breaking waves ahead of them. As they slipped and stumbled their way through the shifting sand to the water, David couldn't help but internally laugh at his current situation. Twenty minutes ago, they were in

143

his den talking about angels and crystal spheres, and now he was walking with this beautiful woman on the beach, like two lovers on a first date. *I am pretty sure this is the point where I wake up!*

***

The light was fading, as the sun had set behind the mountains to the west. It was taking with it the multicolor of the day and leaving the slightly monochromic world of a thousand shades of gray in its place. It was the time of day when features began to blur into the background and reflections of the daylight dulled into shadows.

As they strolled up the beach arm in arm, watching the passing of another day, Lorenza stopped to pick up a small seashell—a nautilus. She held it between her fingers, looked carefully at one end of it, and then handed it to David. She pointed to the end she had been studying. "Do you see that? The signature of all creation was encapsulated in that shell. One of the secrets of the universe made up of calcium and other materials, yet perfect every time." She continued to walk a little farther up the beach as David stood there looking down at the seashell, clearly missing something she had seen.

"I see a seashell. What else is there to see?" He quickly walked up next to her as they continued to move northward.

"There is the story of everything on that little mollusk; all of creation is held within that shell.

Every atom in all galaxies contains the same pattern. It is created with a code inside to replicate itself like all others in its class. Each cell comes together in a particular sequence to form a pattern that cannot be unseen once recognized; each aspect of life." Lorenza slipped away from him and looked up and saw a star. She closed her eyes, and her lips moved in silence. She then gently pulled on his arm and continued walking.

"What was that?" David enquired.

"The first star at night is the one I always make my wish on. I have since I was a young girl. My uncle taught me to do that, and I have never stopped." She smiled and retook his arm, shivering slightly. David took off his jacket and laid it around her shoulders. "I should have brought a sweater, I think." She pulled in closer to him. "Have you never made a wish, David?"

"Not since my tenth birthday. I guess my take on it is that..." David paused and reflected on his words for a moment, "All of it is already in place, and wishing or hoping this would happen or that, wouldn't change anything." David was still holding the seashell. "What was this about?" He held the seashell out to her.

Lorenza looked at the shell and then looked at the sand in front of her, which appeared to glow as the evening became darker. "I will answer that, if you agree to answer one simple question of mine afterward?" She smiled up into his face. "Deal?"

"Deal." David nodded and then pointed to the shell in his hand. "So why the deep and abiding respect for seashells? Are you a member of some secret society using them as totems or ritual objects?"

"No, I am not a member of some, what did you call it, *secret society*. It is more a guild." Lorenza laughed. "Some of the first human drawings discovered are of this pattern reflecting the circle starting at the center and then moving outward in concentric rings; each spiral making the picture more significant and more extensive. It is the symbol of all unity in the universe. If you look at the shell, you will see where it starts and how it grows outward, expanding and getting larger. You will notice the growth pattern is *nearly* identical to the next one you pick up. However, you need to look no further than down at your fingertips to see it appear once again. In many ancient cultures, the spiral depicts the path leading the soul to evolve, and ultimately obtain absolute knowledge: *the path of enlightenment*.

"I thought you were a lit major. You must have been reading more than *The Divine Comedy* in grad school." David shook his head, then turned and started back to the staircase that began their journey. "Okay, your turn. Ask away."

"So, Mr. David, tell me, where did all of this come from?" She waved her hand at the darkening sky over them and then retook his hand and continued to walk.

146

"Oh, no simple question like where did I grow up or when did I get my first bicycle? Just straight to 'tell me how the universe was formed'."

Lorenza laughed and bumped him with her hip. "No, really, I want to know your thoughts on this."

David paused for a moment, contemplating where to begin his answer. As they continued walking, he opened with, "Being a man of science as I am, I hold to the belief all of this was created through purely natural processes of atomic energy, matter, and all the rules that govern the complete universe. Reductionism tells us it all started with the Big Bang, and science has done a good job of proving that back in time to maybe just one or two seconds before the whole system came into existence. This started the expansion processes, compressing gas into solids, creating the rules by which all elements must function—leading up to the long, endless process of life starting and stopping to arrange itself into the forms of simple proteins or single-cell organisms that could regenerate, reproduce, and collect into larger and more complex systems. The mutation is caused by atomic particles displacing a gene here, a chromosome there, and we end up with talking apes that can have abstract thoughts. I guess that is the closest I can give you regarding how all of this came to be."

Lorenza stopped walking and looked down. Then she looked up at David. "It is the two seconds in your explanation that concern me. Those just before the universe came into existence and what you refer to as your laws governing it." She smiled at him.

"What do you mean? This isn't the part where you introduce me to God as the primary mover, and all the rest is just physics, is it?" He chuckled. David felt her hand tighten in his as if he had hit a nerve and felt its reflex.

"Do you know how much energy there is in the universe right now?" She spoke very slowly to make sure her accent did not distort her words at all.

"No idea, but a lot, I am sure." David wondered where this was going.

"The equation is something like one point five-six times ten to the ten-thousandth power in watts of energy. Like you said, 'a lot.' The mass is almost beyond calculation, and that does not consider the reality of dark matter if it exists. Yet all of that, according to your rules of science, came into existence in less than one ten-thousandth of a millisecond and then expanded, creating both time and space. Your own Mr. Einstein says that cannot happen. The Laws of Thermodynamics clearly state energy cannot be created nor destroyed. Yet, that is the prevailing scientific explanation. Then, one must ask, what is the universe? A huge void? In what exactly? Or is it just there, and we need to accept that because it is.

"One can pack a classroom or auditorium with thousands of people to hear 'an expert' speak about the scientific principles behind the causation of something out of nothing that ends up in direct

148

contradiction of other well-established scientific principles. Yet, take those same people and have a priest discuss the concept of creation according to religious beliefs. They are all anxiously awaiting the ending to get home and watch the next sporting event on television. Is there really any difference?" She slowly took her hand away and started to climb up the staircase, holding her shoes in one hand and the handrail in the other.

David stood for a moment still on the sand, processing her remarks. Suddenly he was feeling something inside of him react to them. It was not his logic that was working, but something else that had resonated within him as she had spoken. He had never looked at his beliefs in that way. *The two seconds.* He saw no reason to argue the point, as she was not trying to sell him on anything. She was just stating her view and where her logic came from. Any statement he made in opposition to her view would only be out of ego and not of the intricate thought process he would generally use to solve a complex problem. The bottom line was he didn't know the answer to her question, but he couldn't shake the strange feeling he may soon find out. David looked up the stairway and then began his climb, taking the steps two at a time.

Chapter 17

David walked down the stairs in his grey sweats and a black T-shirt. The wind had picked up during the night, and on this morning, the rain was pelting the ocean side of the house. Not an unusual storm for this time of year, but one he had not expected. He was in great need of a coffee, as his blood-caffeine level had fallen below the danger limit, and he needed to rejuvenate himself with at least two full cups with sugar. As he made his way to the kitchen, he noticed the light in his office and stuck his head inside.

Lorenza was sitting in his oversized leather chair, wrapped in a comforter, and her face buried in an old text she had found.

"Good morning. I hope the spare bedroom met your five-star approval. Sleep well?" David asked, not wanting to invade her space too much yet this morning.

"Terrible. I really couldn't get back to sleep after four. Jetlag, I presume. So, I thought I would peruse your library. Very interesting for the most part. Not unusual for a writer and therapist, except for those two shelves over there." Lorenza pointed to the bookshelf to the left of the window. "Those are of an entirely different sort, and somehow, I did not expect anything like that here." She held up the book she was reading with an extravagantly decorated spine. *In Quaerere de Occulta* by Alvarado Sallolari, Florence 1561. "This book deserves to be in a special library, not collecting dust and mold here on a shelf. The value of this book is quite substantial from a commercial standpoint, and the knowledge within it borders on pure heresy and paganism."

"I need a cup of coffee...want one?" David wasn't yet ready for academic discourse on authors and obscure books.

"I have one, thank you. I did what you told me to do; I made myself at home. Making coffee is one of the special things I like to do in the kitchen." She smiled at him.

Coming back into the room, David pulled out the chair from his desk and turned it so he could see

Lorenza. Her eyes had dropped back to the book and some papers she had on her lap. Her lips moved silently and slowly with every word she read as if it were some kind of treasure worth saving. Across the room, he could tell they were handwritten and aged some by the discoloration of the paper.

"I must be honest. I have had that book for maybe three years now, and I have never opened it. Albert, Father Kennedy, gave it to me along with most of the others on that shelf. He told me one day, it might come in handy. I accepted it more out of respect than anything else. I read the title and just put it up there, thinking someday I may see what it had to offer. But like so many Renaissance books, written in codes and ciphers, I just never had the time for that sort of thing. You know, doing my writing and all."

"David, it was written in code because this book was never meant for circulation but was to be kept within a very close circle of those that were, for lack of a better word, *initiates*. Alvarado Sallolari was an extraordinary character, living on the edge of the Renaissance movement, yet was consulted by many who wanted a hand up, if you will, in the society in Florence. Rich and withdrawn, he rubbed shoulders with everyone of any importance but kept his own life very private and partly hidden from view behind the seven-foot walls of his villa. Little is known about him. Just that there were two camps built around him—one that worshiped him and another that wanted to see him in front of the Dominicans,

153

answering questions of faith for the writing of the book. *This* book." Lorenza held it up.

David looked at her with surprise. "*That* book?"

"My real questions are how did your Father Kennedy happen to have it in his possession? and why did he pass it on to you, with some cryptic reference? Additionally, it appears the good Father was only interested in one section of the book. He thought it important enough to put a bookmark at the beginning and the end of the segment. The section about the Zohakers."

"Never heard of them, honestly." David was trying to concentrate on what she was saying, but too many random thoughts were inundating his mind, and he was having a hard time focusing on any one of them.

"Not surprising really. Even scholars of Middle Eastern studies have only heard of them, and no one up to today has ever read anything about them since *this* book was published four hundred years ago and purportedly lost. Apparently, not only did Father Kennedy know about them, but he also attempted to translate one of their most sacred and obscure prayers. He explains all of this in the margin notes." She picked up her coffee cup and sipped it. "Tell me, did he study comparative religions of the Middle East at any time?"

Some threads of understanding were beginning to come together within David's mind, and he realized he was starting to hone in on something important. If Kennedy had found something

154

important, it had to do with his work. Giving it to David meant he wanted him to see something. *But what exactly?*

"Would you mind giving me the cliff-notes version of what this means? I don't believe my brain has been up long enough to absorb the whole dissertation." David stood up, left the room, and then came back with the coffee pot and proceeded to fill both of their cups. He set the pot on a side table, as it was almost empty anyway.

Lorenza explained. "David, we are talking about an ancient people. Most likely about ten to twelve thousand years ago. They were civilized, living in collective communities, domesticating animals, and growing grains and fruits. They had also somehow learned metalworking when most of the world was still using stones. The legends we have gathered tell us they lived in the lower east side of Caucasus. Maybe three or four small city-states. They were monotheistic in their views."

"Wow, that seems way too early for that kind of thought processing. How could they have pulled that together? A charismatic leader? It takes Zoroaster another couple of thousand years to start up that idea, right?" David asked, not entirely sure how he knew that. *College history class, I guess.* He didn't consider the question too long.

"We have reason to believe they existed and in this way from other extant texts that came later, which allude to them and their beliefs. In some of the earliest Sanskrit records, they speak of the people of the Diwali, *the bringer of light* or *glower of light*. They mention the Zohak by name within a couple of sutras. Later, as the Zoroastrians you mentioned begin to expand their territorial footprint in size and strength, it makes sense they would want to conquer the Zohak people for the value of their knowledge alone. But they don't. Very surprising since the Persians could have put a hundred men in the field for every single Zohakian man. And yet, they didn't. The Zoroastrian writings speak of fear and terror when describing the Zohakians."

"Why is that?" David asked, now finding himself riveted by Lorenza's story.

"For on their side, they had Angra Mainyu," Lorenza continued. "Prince of Darkness, an adverse spirit that taught them advanced military methods, metal making, and other *darker tactics.*"

"*Darker Tactics,*" David repeated with the same emphasis.

"The prayer Father Kennedy translated, from some unknown source, is apparently, a prayer for protection in times of war. It is called, as best as it can be translated, *The Prayer of Him Who Waits and Is Hidden.* It consists of fourteen lines and is done in a boustrophedon pattern, what used to be called the snake pattern, as it a style of writing in which one line is read left to right, the line below it read right to left, and so forth. This is in contrast with European languages, in which lines always begin on the same side, usually the left, and are read to the right.

"It is still in fragments as would be expected due to it being translated by someone who did not know the base language, but from several other language groups, it appears Kennedy traced back enough of the words to give a general overview of the story." She paused and picked up the other piece of paper. She looked at David and waited. He finally nodded for her to go ahead.

"At the time...Some battle occurred...Souls lost forever but without regard, for no one would...to the clay that life was breathed into...Before the end.

"...*Five masters* (leaders or principals) left without harm or defeat...One came to where we now stand... The First Messenger (angel?) that brought the Black Flame with...He shall always be with us in times...strife and no one shall mourn their fallen...with him."

"Lucifer?" David asked, wondering if this was a pagan religion dedicated to the bringer of light, the morning star.

"No, I don't believe so. Another equal in importance and strength, but not Lucifer. *One of five* is the interesting part. May I take this book back to Venice with me and show it to someone of great importance there?" She replaced the papers inside it and shut the book gently.

"Don't you mean Rome? To the Vatican?"

"No. Based on Father Kennedy's letter and some of these other notations, I think it would be best if someone else looked at this." Lorenza said, looking a little concerned.

"Of course. It is still all Greek to me, and I am unsure what to make of it. Kennedy never had two quarters to rub together personally, so how he could have even afforded that kind of book is a mystery all on its own. But not only that, he obviously studied it. He began to make some sense of it. Perhaps he found a lead to what he was looking for his whole life. The reason behind possessions and the existence of demons." David shrugged for a moment and then thought it through a little more. "But I do want the book back, agreed?"

"Of course, it is yours, and I shall make sure it is returned to you undamaged."

She looked into his eyes and smiled that lovely smile of hers and David felt himself melting again. "Alternatively," Lorenza said, now appearing to have a mischievous look about her, "you could accompany me to Venice. That is, if you aren't too busy at the moment."

David looked at her, trying to determine if she was serious. He then reflected on his current situation. Outside of Ralph, he did not have any binding obligations. No service was going to be held for Kennedy, per orders from the Church. No eulogies needed to be conducted. He looked around his office—looked at Lorenza and at the book she was now holding. He then looked towards the safe, which housed the *other* book. "I imagine if I say yes, you will want me to bring that one as well?" He motioned his head toward the safe.

158

Lorenza glanced in that direction, then turned back to David. "Well, we can't leave it here."

Chapter 18

In a lavish apartment, within the walls of Vatican City, Cardinal Antoine Baptist Zimmerman was hanging up a phone. The office was illuminated by a single lamp that arched just over his chair. His mind raced, trying to pull all the variables together. Too many loose ends needed tidying up right now, and the fallback position had to be prepared. Each step had been planned so carefully for so long. Every detail accounted for years of planning and yet this, now.

The cardinal swiveled in his chair to face the large window. It was pitch dark outside; the lights of Vatican City were reflected on the glass. Beyond that, was the stinking city he both loved and hated so much. It felt as if it left a sour taste in his throat. If only he could shut it off, like a switch. *Where was the off button?*

The apartment was on the top floor, a penthouse, giving him the best views of the seemingly never-ending city. He turned again and leaned his elbows on the table. The table was cluttered with files about the demon book. The files were there to keep him up to date on the daily developments in the search for the book. His eyes landed on the one he was looking for. The paper clutched in his fingers creased from too much handling. *We are too close for all to be lost.*

He turned from the table, his mind elsewhere. The clock of St Peter's chimed, the noise like hammering on his brain. It was the deepest of tones, summoning him back to the reality of his desk.

A fragile moment of quiet arrived. It was brief and followed by a slight knock on his chamber door. Cardinal Zimmerman exhaled deeply. "Come in." The door was opened, and another man of the red and white entered. He bowed to the sitting Cardinal and then took a seat across from him.

"There is a problem in America." Cardinal Santorini stated. "A rather large one."

"I too, have just been made aware of that fact, brother." Zimmerman turned and looked out the window. "It appears our Father Kennedy is dead. And self-inflicted at that. Our 'consultant' has

162

reported she believes the book is now in the care of another, a therapist of some sort."

"Did she find him?" Santorini inquired.

"That, my brother, is a question that concerns me greatly. We last heard from Dr. Pellegrini three days ago when she provided us with the news on Kennedy and her suspicion regarding who may have the book. After that, she went completely silent and has been unresponsive to our communications. It now appears she is on her way back to Italy; however, she is not headed to Rome, but rather Venice. And it seems she is not traveling alone. Dr. Wright is traveling with her." Zimmerman paused and looked at his clenched ancient hands. "Let us be sure when they arrive, a reception is awaiting them at the airport."

***

As David sat in his seat on the flight, Lorenza was asleep next to him. Looking around the cabin, David noticed most of the other passengers were sleeping as well. He thumbed through the book and found a note folded inside written by Cardinal Brambilla. As he read it, his head shook in disbelief.

Dear Antoine,

I have been busy attempting a way to destroy the book and I've given up on it. You may have noticed the storm which began abruptly last night – that resulted from my actions. Each time I attempted to tear a page from the book, lightning and thunder occurred as if the book had a will of its own. It doesn't matter how much of a believer you are in such things, understand that this book truly has unknown powers.

I am afraid its destruction is not simple. It guards itself and resists harm. That is the case with two pages I tore out, which are still inside the book. As soon as I did, blood began gushing from my ear. There is something amiss about this book. I have resigned myself to the belief there is no way to destroy it. You must understand this.

I will now take responsibility for its custody.

With my deepest regrets,

Matteo

David folded the note and placed it back in the book. He contemplated Brambilla's words. *I wonder why he never sent.* David flipped to a random page in the book and ever so slightly began tearing at the top of it. The plane jerked wildly.

Over the plane's intercom system, he heard a click followed by the voice of the captain blare through the cabin. "Folks, we are currently experiencing some unexpected turbulence. Please be so kind to remain in your seats until things settle a bit. Flight crew, please discontinue any inflight services for the time being."

Next to him, he heard Lorenza groggily ask, "Is everything ok?"

"Just some turbulence," David said, staring down at the book. *A very odd coincidence.*

Chapter 19

The Venice Marco Polo Airport is the third busiest airport in Italy and connects more than 13 million travelers a year to the iconic canals and Byzantine-influenced architecture. The terminal is not only architecturally stunning but is also equipped with a state-of-the-art security system. As passengers de-board and make their way through Customs, their complete biometric details are captured through a facial scan and checked against the passenger's travel documents and cross-referenced against border authority databases and other law enforcement records...including those of the Vatican Police.

As David and Lorenza made their way through the line at Customs, David was first to reach the official requesting his passport. He handed his documents to the young woman in the bullet-proof glass booth and answered her three questions as she scanned his passport. Her smile faded as she typed a numeric code into the computer. Looking up at him again, she had replaced her smile with the face of a highly trained security officer.

"It will be just a moment; I need to check something before allowing you to enter." The words flowed out like a well-rehearsed phrase, and had David been a professional smuggler, he would've known he had just been identified. But for David the academic, it was just another annoyance one encounters when traveling in post 9-11 world. However, a few moments later, David felt someone approach him, and he turned to discover a middle-aged man wearing a black suit and tie standing beside him, apparently waiting for the agent to hand him back his passport. Over the man's jacket pocket, he wore his identification, which clearly stated he was an inspector of the National Police Force and not associated with the Customs Office at Marco Polo.

"Your first time in Venice, Dr. Wright?" He asked with slightly accented English. He was a short man, well-built with a hardness in his face suggesting he was prepared to respond to any situation, no matter how far it escalated.

"Yes. I have been to Italy several times but never to Venice." David searched for a smile to relieve the tension coursing through his body.

"There seems to be a matter we need to resolve before we can let you enter our country at this time. Mostly formalities, but we must all adhere to the rules others have set out for us. I'm sure you understand." The investigator forced a smile. "If you would be so kind as to come with me. We'll go someplace where we may speak in private." The man motioned toward the Customs office, which had several windows overlooking the checkpoint.

As David and the investigator moved from the Customs line to the office, Lorenza called out in her native tongue, "I need to come as well." She briskly followed the two men and handed her business card to the investigator, who glanced at it and then smiled.

"I'm lucky today," he yelled back over his shoulder. "You were also on the list of people we're very interested in speaking with. Thanks, Doctor. Please, do come with us. Your expertise, I am sure, will be needed."

In addition to the investigator, David noticed two other men moving behind them through the mass of people. *What in the hell is this all about?*

The officers led them into the room and left them alone. The room was like any other interrogation room in most modern countries: simple, square, with a few hard chairs and a long table with David's and Lorenza's luggage stacked on

169

top it. Three of the four walls were empty except for floor-to-ceiling acoustical tile, and the square tile floor was cleaner and shinier than most hospital wards. The fourth wall held a three-by-four-foot mirror made of reciprocal glass enabling someone on the other side to watch and record them. The obligatory CCTV camera on the wall overlooking the room with the small, red LED light illuminated indicating the room was being recorded.

David smiled, and Lorenza knew precisely why. This was the sweating period that was the bread and butter of all law enforcement; the officers hoped the two would concoct some story about why they were together and what they were doing here. Aware of those tactics, David used the time to make some notes in the book he carried with him, and Lorenza followed suit, both appearing like none of this mattered to either of them. David's stomach churned, but this was not the time or place to exhibit any signs of nervousness or fear. The appearance of being annoyed would be natural but accepting it and continuing with one's work would be disheartening to those watching on the other side of the glass and also lessen the waiting time to uncover the real reason they had been detained. Both David and Lorenza were already aware without saying anything why they were pulled in. The book, or books.

The door opened, and the investigator entered the room, alone and without his jacket. He motioned for them to stay seated as he pulled out a chair and sat down at the table. On his hip, he had a 9mm

170

Beretta model 92 service automatic pistol and in the small of his back was a leather case holding a set of handcuffs. David almost laughed but thought better of it. Stage dressing for what would come next. The display was designed to intimidate and demonstrate authority.

Despite the fact David's and Lorenza's computers and cell phones had been confiscated when they'd entered the room, Lorenza had managed to send off a message before then, when she first suspected trouble. That message would have its effect in less than an hour. She looked at her wristwatch and realized they needed to kill another fifteen minutes.

"I am Inspector Gino Carrari of the National Police. You were stopped because of an urgent dispatch from my headquarters in Rome. It seems someone believes you have a certain item that was taken without permission from the Vatican. They request us to see if you had such an item with you. Just a formality, I assure you." *Clever*, Lorenza thought to herself. Not saying something was stolen, but "taken without permission" — the same thing, essentially, but without accusation. *They have clearly been keeping track of my whereabouts. Evidently, my services are no longer required.*

"What do you – or whoever – think we have that belongs to the Church?" David asked.

"A book. A special and old book that was taken from the Vatican library several years ago, and it's believed it has been given to you by the person

171

responsible for its removal." Carrari hesitated. "Are you in possession of such a book, and do you have it with you?"

"I have a book I recently received. I am not sure of its nature, contents, or value. Dr. Pellegrini and I were working on another book I have had in my family for years to determine its author and place of publication. That is why we are here together. She needed to use her reference library to compare print and paper styles to see if it fits the period it indicates. If it does, she believes the Vatican would most likely desire it for their collection, and she would be the one to determine that for them." David chose each word carefully and with purpose. This was not the time for the idle comment or colloquialism. "May I?" David motioned toward his luggage.

"Please do." Carrari moved so he could better see inside the luggage.

David opened it and took out the book Albert had worried so much about. As he handed it to Carrari, he did so as if it were some paperback novel he'd bought for the flight, something of little value to him or anyone in general.

Carrari ran his hand over it. He looked first at the bare spine and then opened it to the first fly page, where he noticed the strange inscription.

"*Iam enim unus anathema- no venit maranatha,*" he read. "You are already in a state of excommunication from the church, and he will not---" He trailed off. "I don't know that word. Maranatha?"

"Your Latin is quite good for a police officer, Inspector." Lorenza smiled at him. "The last word is not Latin but Aramaic. The inscription reads, 'Praise your Lord, for he is not coming back to you' in a mixture of Latin and Aramaic. It's a curse placed in the front of the book to warn off those who would think of stealing it."

"I learned my Latin in seminary. I had studied to be a priest but found I had a different path to follow. Why would someone use that word in a curse?" He seems genuinely perplexed.

"The word itself is pre-Christian, and the text is far older. It's not about the Church or the Faith. Did you say the item was *stolen* from the Vatican library? I don't remember if you did." Lorenza looked puzzled, and David was once more impressed by her acting skills.

"No, I didn't say that. Why?" Carrari pulled down the glasses he had put on to read. Lorenza glanced at her watch again like she knew precisely what was going to happen next. The door opened as one of the young police officers entered the room and whispered something to Carrari.

"Here? Now?" He looked at the young man, let out a sigh of exasperation, and nodded to him. "Of course, don't keep him waiting."

"It would seem you missed an important appointment with someone, and they are not happy about it at all, Doctor." When Carrari opened the door, a man in his fifties with perfectly combed silver hair, an expensive suit, and several pieces of gold jewelry on his wrist and rings came in. He passed by Carrari without acknowledgment and went straight to Lorenza, took her hand, and kissed it.

"What are you doing here? We had reservations at the palace. What is this about?" He looked at Carrari with a fiery stare. "Do you wish to start to explain yourself?"

"Chief Magistrate, I received orders from Rome to detain this man and check for a lost item from the Vatican. He was traveling with the doctor, so she volunteered to come here with him." Carrari tried to act indifferent, but David could tell he was walking on eggshells. Clearly, Lorenza's acquaintance was not a man to trifle with. If Carrari weren't careful, the Chief Magistrate could make sure Carrari would spend his days checking bags in the customs line.

Turning to David, he said, "That means you are Dr. David Wright, the famous psychoanalyst and author so many people hate. What an honor. Luwegi Monstansanio, Chief Magistrate and Judge of the High Court of Venice. A pleasure." The Magistrate bowed from the waist and took David's hand, which he shook as an old friend would. A dark shadow passed over Carrari's face; that greeting told him everything he needed to know. He wasn't going to win this one; a tie was the best he could hope for right now.

"Inspector. Can you explain to me why these people are being held in a common interrogation room normally reserved for criminals?" Each word hit like a hammer.

"General practice on our part, your Honor. It was only for a short time while we cleared this matter up." Carrari ineffectively tried to appear indifferent.

"A short time. I had time to receive Lorenza's message, take a boat from my office to the railroad station, and have my driver bring me here. You call that a 'short time'? I'm sure your supervisors would be interested to hear about this breach in etiquette you have shown to one of our most prestigious citizens and to a fine American scholar who is generally held in high esteem. I just hope the papers and news services don't find out about this, for then surely someone's head will be on the block." There was no misunderstanding his intent.

"I do apologize for the inconvenience, but it seems Dr. Wright has the book which this bulletin refers to." Carrari handed him the notice and description of the book coming from Rome. Monstansanio looked through it and shrugged as if to say, "so what?"

"Rather vague, wouldn't you say, Inspector?" Monstansanio compared the bulletin to the book he thumbed through and then handed them both back to Carrari.

"Fill out and give Dr. Wright a receipt. Send this to Rome and tell them I want to see the validation from the Vatican this book is theirs sent to me personally. They have four weeks only, and I shall issue a court order demanding its return to Dr. Wright. Understood?" Carrari nodded his understanding and then stepped forward to finish looking through David's luggage.

"Exactly what are you doing?" Luwegi asked him.

"Seeing if he has any other books." Carrari looked at the judge and realized he had just made a colossal error in judgment. Carrari stepped back, hands raised. "Most sorry. Please now, you may leave with the Chief Magistrate with our blessings and thanks for your cooperation." He motioned for the two officers in the hallway to take the bags outside.

In the hallway, after their phones and laptops were returned to them, Lorenza said under her breath, "I am sorry, David, we just lost the book." David smiled like the cat that ate the canary.

"What is it?" Lorenza asked, failing to find any humor in the situation.

"I can't sleep on airplanes. Never could. So, while you were peacefully passed out next to me, I took detailed pictures of the book and each page of the book with my phone. Kennedy's note expressly said not to get the pages out of order, and I wanted to make sure we had their original sequence documented. I also thought having them digitally may come in handy."

Lorenza laughed. "Well, aren't you just full of surprises, Dr. Wright?"

Chapter 20

Venice Santa Lucia is the central station on the island of Venice, located just off the Grand Canal. Upon arriving at Venice Santa Lucia station at the west end of the lagoon on which the city is built, transportation is generally limited to private boats, ferries, and walking within the city itself. After saying their goodbyes and declaring their thanks to the Chief Magistrate, who had to continue to Verona on other business, Lorenza and David walked to the public area where private boats awaited their commuters. A beautiful mahogany and chrome cruiser was sitting at one of the tie-ups. A handsome young man was polishing the chrome with a rag, while joking with another boat chauffeur nearby. Turning as he saw Lorenza, his entire face lit up, reflecting a massive smile as he waved to her. He hurried to make his way over to take her bag and David's as well. He placed the heavy loads onto the craft effortlessly and then helped each of them aboard.

"David, meet Carlos. Carlos lives in the Master's house with us. He is our boat chauffeur and our jack of all trades, who makes sure we say our prayers at night and don't swear too much during the day. Maria, who you will meet later at the house, is Carlos's sister. I will warn you now: do not, under any circumstances, play any card games with either of them. They both are of Medici bloodlines, and they know all the tricks in the world that can be performed with cards designed to separate people from their money. Not that they need any; it is just good sport to them.

"You are so bad. You must not say that about me. He's American, are you not?" Carlos smiled at David, who nodded his head yes. "Then he will be fair game. All Americans love to gamble; I have seen that in movies." He nodded and laughed. "Home?" He looked at Lorenza, who nodded yes.

As they pulled out into the Grand Canal, David sat back and noticed other people observing them. It took him a moment to realize the people who were staring at them were not tourists but locals. They recognized the boat and the driver, and that meant something to them.

"It is a shame we lost the book that meant so much to Father Kennedy, but you mentioned you have photos on your phone?" Lorenza was not looking at him, but watching the water pass the boat. Small white waves from the bow were dancing with sunlight on them.

"I do, so all is not lost. We still have the textual material." David's heart sank a little as he thought about what the book must have meant to Kennedy in a much more personal way.

"Do you trust me, David?" Lorenza turned and looked him directly in the eyes.

"I believe I do. Why?" David was trying to find an answer that was not there. What a strange question at this point.

"Can you send me the photos in the order they were taken?" She opened her shoulder bag and pulled out her phone.

"Alright. Are you going to tell me why?" David was scrolling through his phone.

Waiting for it to boot up, she was still silent on his last question.

"The why is because you trust me." She smiled at him. "Trust is trust." David began sending the photos to her phone.

"Carlos," Lorenza called out, and the man turned to look at her. "Vercelli's"

Carlos nodded and made the boat perform a one hundred and eighty-degree turn in the canal and head back up from where they had just come. He then took the craft down several side canals until

David was utterly lost. Then, Carlos pulled the boat up to a mooring, jumped out, and tied it up. The building was four stories tall, whitewashed, and had seen better days. On top, it had a red-tiled roof and some weeds growing out of the gutters around the edge. Some of the windows appeared to have been painted on the inside so only a reflection was seen of the canal and the dancing water. David guessed the green shutters by each window had last seen paint about twenty years ago. There was no plaque on the door, nor was there a house number. Even though the house stated nothing of importance about itself, David felt it carried a great deal of importance inside.

Carlos ran back and helped Lorenza get ashore onto the stone walkway running the length of the canal. David started to follow, but Carlos put a hand on his shoulder. "Not wise, my new friend. They do not know you, which means you could be trouble. Just sit here, and we can chat while the good doctor does what she must do here. They know her well." Carlos never stopped smiling at him. He was very disarming in his warmth but also firm and overpowering in his own way. David sat back and waited. Carlos pulled out a map and showed him where they were and how they had gotten there and pointed to the location of the Master's house, which they would be headed to next. David was still lost.

Ten minutes later, Lorenza returned, and Carlos helped her back into the boat. She sat down and smiled at David. Carlos had them back on a different canal in just a few minutes and then moved them around to where they re-emerged out onto the Grand Canal once more. David was now even more turned around and initially thought they were heading back to the railway station.

"Do you trust me?" David asked Lorenza, who was smiling at him.

"Of course, I do. It is just that there are some things you should not know about, and that house is one of them. That family has been forgers for over four hundred years, father to son. They have created some of the best forgeries in the world, and if you were to glimpse inside, you would not want to leave. Row upon row of ancient texts all produced right here. I gave them the electronic files, and they downloaded them onto their systems in seconds. They traded in their printing presses years ago for much more modern technology that can replicate any typeface and ink. They have rooms filled with paper that has been around for hundreds of years in preparation for future needs. They have optical character readers and sophisticated computer systems used solely to reproduce missing pieces to puzzles. Inside are vats of ink that have been continuously blending for hundreds of years. A device that imprints each letter into the paper like a press would have done centuries ago. Their work is so accurate most experts can't find any errors in it. I picked leather as close to the original colors as I could find and then told them to varnish and burnish it to the point it will look like the real thing. Within forty-eight hours, we will have a near-identical copy of Father Kennedy's book sitting at the house. That is why you would have never made it past the front entry hall. They are very protective, and now I have shared with you one of the protected secrets in all of Venice. I suggest you now forget it." She picked up his hand and kissed it gently.

"What does something like that cost?" David was simultaneously amazed, appalled, and overwhelmed.

"More than what most people make in five years of hard work. And worth every penny of it."

They moved down a side canal, and David sat in quiet amazement; this city had so many secrets no one knew. Where does one start, and how does one learn all of this? Puzzles, games, riddles, and fear had become some of his closest associates now. Those, and the woman sitting next to him, with the smiling eyes and gifted mind.

Chapter 21

Dr. Marcel Rothe loved his job. Born in Rome fifty-three years ago, he had been raised within the Church. His family attended every service they could at Saint Peter's. From the time he was a small child, he knew his calling was to one day work inside the pristine walls of Vatican City. After graduating *scuola superiore*, he attended Sapienza, more formally known as The Sapienza University of Rome, before receiving his doctorate in religious politics from the Pontifical University of the Holy Cross when he was twenty-seven. While still in school, a bishop had recommended him for a position as a messenger inside the facility. From there, he moved into an apprentice position for those in the Information Service Section—the folks who ran the daily news and administrated the short-wave radio station, Radio Vatican City. His clear, concise, and error-free copywriting abilities had been noted by many of the high-ranking members of the Curia, and letters of appreciation began filling his file. Upon graduating, he secured a position in the Diplomatic Office, whereby he was responsible for dealing with many foreign ambassadors and legations seeking aid from the Vatican. At that time, he had been one of the twenty-four hundred people working within the borders of the Stato Della Città del Vaticano, *Vatican City*

Over the years, many eyes watched his impressive rise in status and envied him. Marcel was simultaneously smooth, careful, charming, and calculating. When Jorge Mario Bergoglio became the sitting Pope, Marcel received the tap to be the *Prime Legate for Affairs for His Holiness*. Along with the prestigious title, Rothe was also given privileges few ever receive. He became one of sixty-two people—not part of the clergy—living inside the city's walls. Marcel had his own apartment in the Papal Palace, a car and driver, and a housekeeper would come in during the days to clean, wash, and make sure everything was in order. He had 'the black card' from American Express, two passports, and was considered untouchable because of his diplomatic immunity.

He was single, aloof, and not above doing favors for those in the ruling class, as long it meant a personal acknowledgment or an increase in his bank account. He viewed himself as the 'fixer' for the Church in Rome and the architect of a one-person intelligence service for anyone who could cross his hands with silver. He was pretty good at it too.

Rothe had been noticing for months the behavior of certain members of the Curia were changing, and there appeared to be a new faction forming within the inner circles. It seemed to be centered around Cardinal Zimmerman, one of the few men who voiced his desire to be the next person to sit in the Chair of Peter and who openly criticized the current 'administration.' Even though there was no indication the current Pope had any illnesses or reason for leaving his position, it seemed like Zimmerman was preparing for an immediate change in leadership. When all of this started, Rothe was one of the first to find favor in Zimmerman's eyes. It was made clear to him, if he played along with the cardinal, he would most likely stay in his current position after any transition happened. 'Playing along' meant both answering questions and then asking questions of others, additionally providing small services were within his sphere of influence.

He had not considered it unusual when the cardinal had come to him and asked him to contact the National Police and put out a request to obtain a book from an American who somehow had gotten ahold of it; the cardinal had relayed to him it belonged in the Special Collections of the Vatican Library. Neither was he taken aback by the request to manufacture documentation proving the proof it belonged to the Church. It simply required a certification letter bearing Marcel's signature stating as much.

As he walked down the hallway with its heavy drapes and gold trimmings, he was highly pleased with himself this task had been so effortless. Detective Carrari had brought it to his office. Carrari, upon being handed Marcel's document of ownership, read it, nodded his approval, and left. Now Marcel was holding the book still inside the police wrapper to be delivered personally to the cardinal.

Cardinal Zimmerman was standing in the hallway in front of his office, talking to another member of the College. Cardinal Santorini, the secretary for the Curia. Both men seemed deeply engaged in a private and somewhat hushed conversation. Inferring both men currently wanted privacy, Marcel made his way toward a balcony overlooking the foyer below. From there, he watched the comings and goings of assistants and other priests all part of the organization keeping Vatican City running. Cardinal Zimmerman raised his hand to Santorini and then came over to greet Marcel. He displayed an unusual level of kindness as he asked Marcel how he was doing. The friendliness continued for a few moments, and then Marcel handed Cardinal Zimmerman the package. It appeared to Marcel as if a significant burden had been taken off the cardinal's shoulders as he pulled the book to his chest and held it like a tiny innocent infant. He patted Marcel on the shoulder, thanked him over and over, then winked at him, suggesting his efforts would not go unrewarded.

Marcel nodded and thanked him for allowing him to be of service and then nodded politely to the other cardinal standing a few feet away, who equally dipped his head to Marcel. As he walked away, Marcel felt more secure in his position with this enterprise was out of the way. He imagined it would be another point of recognition at the right time when honors came due.

Chapter 22

By the time David and Lorenza arrived at the villa, David was wiped and didn't have much energy left to look around the home. He was primarily interested in finding a bed in which he could curl up for as long as was needed to get his senses back. International travel caused enough anxiety without the inconvenience of dealing with officials and customs, the entire book travesty at the airport, and being overwhelmed by Venice. He needed to recharge his batteries, and some solid sleep was the only solution.

When he woke up the next day, he looked at his watch and realized he had not yet reset it to the new time zone. He searched for his phone, but because the villa wasn't wired for electricity, he discovered his phone was dead. Therefore, he had to make an approximation as to what time it was. After pulling open the drapes and pushing out the shutters on the window, he was aware it was well past the morning and looked more like afternoon, but he really couldn't tell. *How long did I sleep?*

David also didn't quite know what to make from the idea of sharing this place with a leopard, but Lorenza had gone overboard to explain Aza was an integral part of the household as well as its primary security system. He now wondered why it surprised him so much. Nothing else fit into logical little packages at the moment. *Why shouldn't a leopard be roaming around a house in Venice at night?* How was this so different than having people halfway around the world dispatching the police in search of a book he had only just received from Father Kennedy. Father Kennedy, who lived in a world consisting of demons and ghosts and all things unnatural. *Just par for the course at present*, he thought.

As he studied the room he currently occupied, David realized his internal coffee meter had fallen below the acceptable limit and before doing anything else, he needed his brew to jar the neurons lose in his head.

After his morning ablutions, he dressed casually and descended the steps of the grand spiral towered staircase. David noticed the place was like something out of a medieval movie he had seen.

Once on the main floor, he searched for the kitchen, and upon locating it, he walked in.

Upon seeing it, his mind reeled once more. Here he was in this villa seemingly out of sync with the time flow of the world, yet the kitchen appeared to be something out of *Home and Garden* magazine. *You could run a restaurant out of here.* All stainless-steel appliances, ultra-modern everything. His attempt to locate coffee was cut short by a soft voice behind him.

"It's the only room in the house wired with electricity, but don't tell anyone. If you let me know what it is you want, I will get it for you, Doctor." David turned to see a woman who appeared to be ripped from the pages of some fashion magazine. Maria was standing there in a light blue suit and white blouse. Her silver hair was beautiful against her tanned and healthy-looking skin. Her eyes looked right through him, and he blushed at the way she had appraised him. Like Lorenza, this woman held herself with a certain elegance and grace while holding a perpetual smile exposing the fact, she was currently privy to a lot more information about his surroundings than he was.

"Good morning," David said to her, looking a bit embarrassed and disoriented. "I am David."

"Yes, Dr. Wright, you are, and it is actually afternoon. Therefore, I would imagine you need some coffee and something to eat." Her voice was soft and sweet. Not at all motherly, but more a voice of someone utterly confident in themselves who had nothing to prove to anyone.

"Just coffee. Nothing else. But a large, I mean big cup of coffee." He mined his wishes with his hands as to the size while smiling.

"You wish for a mug of coffee, not a cup. I think that is what you are telling me." She smiled again with a glint in her eye at him, all-knowing.

"Yes, please. And who are you? You can't be part of the staff here." He knew how completely tongue-tied he sounded at the moment, but Maria had overpowered him with her polish and charm, and David had no idea right now how to ask a simple question in this house.

"I am Maria, and I am the shepherd of the flock here. I make certain everyone has what they want and need and ensure the tranquility of our home is not disturbed." She moved across the room and started to do something with a strange-looking device. "It would be best if you went to the study, and I will bring you your coffee shortly. To find it, you will want to go through the door down the hall, and then to the right. The big room is filled with books. Thomas is there, and he will show you around."

"You're kicking me out of your kitchen, aren't you?" David smiled a rather large smile.

"Yes. I am. You are a guest, and you don't belong in a place like this. So please, the study if you don't mind," motioning toward the door.

David nodded and went through the door. Making his turn down at the end of the hall, he walked into a bright-lit library with its floor-to-ceiling windows open, with rows of leather-bound books in the dark hardwood shelving, a remarkable view of Venice, and a leopard lying on a Persian carpet with a very handsome looking man standing in the middle of the whole scene. The man's face was buried in a book. David's book—the one he had brought from Boston with him. Lorenza had already given it to him to examine.

"I've been told it is afternoon, so good afternoon." David walked toward him and extended his hand in friendship. The other man closed the book, pulled off his reading glasses, and reached out to take it.

"Hello, I am Thomas, and you must be David. Dr. Wright is that correct?" The man had one of those smiles that was genuine and warm, carrying a calmness and gentleness about him. From behind him, David heard Maria's voice.

"Here the two of you go." David turned to see Maria walk in with two large mugs of coffee and some cookies on a plate. She placed them down on a table and straightened up. "Thomas, make sure David eats something; otherwise, my coffee will burn a hole through his stomach." She smiled and left them alone again. Both men went to take a cup of coffee, and Thomas motioned for them to take a seat on the couch by the window.

"I am Thomas Morelli, Father Thomas Morelli, a Catholic priest who doesn't do much preaching but who spends most of my time teaching at a Catholic

University and doing research for a book I have spent a good amount of time on. You're the psychoanalyst turned bestselling author, aren't you?" The one appearing to take great pleasure in browbeating the Church?" Thomas smiled and sat back, sipping his coffee.

"That's me. Right up there toward the top of the list of the Vatican's most hated authors." David took one sip of coffee and then looked down into his cup. "How did she make that? That's not just coffee but closer to the nectar of the gods. Wow!"

"I know. I have already determined when I leave here, I will never get another cup of coffee like the ones Maria makes." Now in a slight whisper, Thomas said, "Secretly, I think she uses Holy Water from one of the Churches around here." Thomas laughed at his own joke, which was a pleasure to be seen by David.

"What are all of these?" David moved his hand in the air indicating the rows of books.

"These are some of the rarest manuscripts in the world. Many of these books aren't even known to exist. Many of the books in this library are priceless. The whole room is a treasure trove—an Aladdin's cave, if you will." Thomas put his cup down and walked over to one of the shelves. "I have found books in here I have only seen third-hand references to, and ones scholars ever have claimed no longer exist. I have spent five years researching a book on Giordano Bruno in every conceivable library and special collecting worldwide. Almost everything I collected on him and his writings over those five years, I could have found within this room in less than a week had I been able to start in here first. And that does not even include the fact there are books in this library written by his own hand. It is truly remarkable, and so is the story as to how I arrived here. But that's another story unto itself." Thomas turned and looked at David. "Oh, just listen to me go on. I sound like some lovesick adolescent talking about his first love."

"No, you are fine," David said with a smile. "Your passion is something I have not seen in quite some time in anyone. A scholar wanting to learn for the sake of learning and writing something from the heart is truly powerful."

"Bruno has been my quest since I can't remember when. I was attracted to him in college when I initially started to research him. I became a priest, and many of my teachers tried very hard to move me away from my studies about him, yet they all failed in their attempts." Thomas laughed, lost in thought for a moment. He then reached up and ran his hand down the spine of one of the books. "About five years ago, I started working on a biography of him, and then I got hooked into the case against him. I found myself becoming angry. I couldn't understand how the Church found such fault in him to the point of murdering him." Thomas's face grew flush. "His logic was beyond anything that anyone was applying at the time. His viewpoints were all-encompassing, and his expression in his writing was filled with passion for opening minds to a clear understanding of the universe. Who could find fault in that?"

"Well, it was during the Inquisition, Thomas." David said while sipping from his mug.

"Yes, but Bruno they treated much differently. Do you know that he spent nine lonely years between here and Rome living in the worst cells they could find? They would not let him have books and continued to torture him. And do you know why, David?

"Do tell."

"Because he would not give up an extraordinary truth, a truth he carried with him. It all came down to one book. One very *special* book."

"An extremely rare and special book?" David inquired.

"Indeed. In speaking with Lorenza this morning, it would apparently be the same book taken from you at the airport. She mentioned that you had only just received it from a late friend of yours." Thomas moved across the room and sat behind the desk.

David took the chair across from him and held his cup in his hand. "Father Albert Kennedy. Did you know him?"

"I can't say I did. I read something a few years ago, though, implying he was an exorcist for the Church. The article was vague about him personally and much more about what he had done with some person the Church claimed was possessed." Thomas glanced at the papers on the desk. "I was more interested in the man himself than all the rest of that stuff. He looked to be above it all within the body of the Church. I remember at the time enquiring of the other professors if they knew him and getting quite a cold response from them about him. It seemed he was needed but not wanted within the Church. He taught school as well, didn't he?"

"Catholic school in Boston. All Saints. He was a good teacher, but even the people who worked there were always on edge around him. He was..." David looked for the right words. "Different. Different than most priests. His views would never align well with the standard dogma. In our discussions, he referenced Bruno often claiming he was closer than anyone in understanding the true nature of the universe. He gave me a copy of his book *Cause, Principle and Unity* and had a hard time putting it down."

"The validity of that comment will find no detractors in this room." Thomas smiled. "I find myself becoming more at odds with my church the farther I go into my own research about him and the way the Church treated him. Evidently there was the obvious heretical knowledge they were trying to snuff out, as well as something else they were seeking. Something more along the lines of the 'underground stream' the mystics of the medieval period spoke about. A secret knowledge that in some way ties a lot of different things together."

197

Thomas stood up and began walking in a circle around the desk. "Let's take, for example, alchemy. It really has two aspects. Everyone knows about the transmutation of gold from lead, but also another aspect, which was the manifestation of knowledge neither held nor allowed by the Church. As Carl Jung puts it, some part of our collective consciousness holds a deeper truth and fear within it; an arcane or hidden truth that if we knew it, would certainly set us free in a different sense of the meaning, but that would equally terrify us as humans." Thomas walked toward the window looking out at the boats.

David studied Thomas for a long moment as he decided what felt so familiar about him. Figuring it out, David smiled and said, "You are a lot more like Father Kennedy than you can imagine. How did you come to go into the priesthood?"

"A single promise." Thomas turned and smiled a sad smile. "My father had been a soldier like his father before him. All of them battle born, bred for the crucible of war. We're talking VMI and West Point types of men. Dedicated, hard, and also brilliant. The two of them were military history majors in college. Both commissioned officers in combat units. 'Our family,' my dad used to say, 'doesn't fly desk.' A dinner conversation would be about Lee, Grant, Pershing, and places like Bella Woods and New Market during the civil war. I was eleven when he was killed in combat."

Thomas sat back down at the desk fidgeting with an ink pen. "My mother placed the flag from his coffin, into one of those triangle wooden boxes with the glass front in his office at home, alongside his father's. The night of his formal military funeral, after the color guard and the trumpets had finished playing Taps, my mother made me promise on my love for her I would not become a solider, no matter what happened."

"Fair request, given the current circumstances." David said.

"For sure. A few years later, when I was sixteen, she was diagnosed with later-staged cancer." Thomas's eyes began to fill.

"At night, I would sit and read to her from the Bible for hours. She loved that, and it gave her great comfort. The last few months of her life, she kept hammering on me to hold to the promise I had made years before. My mother knew I loved history, and she could see the same characteristics developing in me that had driven my father. She died a few years later."

"I'm sorry to hear," David said.

"Thank you. By that time, I had found a fascination with church history, which arguably is as violent as military history. So, I went to a Catholic university and took the special program to enter the priesthood. After my ordination, I worked out an agreement with my bishop to continue my education. I got my master's and then a doctorate in history. Upon graduating, others in my diocese determined it would be somewhat of a waste to dispatch me to a parish to perform liturgy on

Sundays, baptism on Saturdays, and running bingo games in the hall on Wednesday nights, so they asked me to start teaching at another Catholic university. I fell in love with it. It's my opinion opening minds is one of the greatest achievements anyone can hope for."

"And Bruno?" David asked.

"And Bruno. As I said, five years ago, I started on a mission to write a biography, and it led me into a whole different realm. After this past spring semester ended, I came to Venice and followed a scent down a path leading me here and in the now. I have my book almost ready to publish that will certainly not earn me credits within the Church. They may even ban it from being published."

"Would they actually do that?" David asked.

"I am not sure. I have considered that and what it would mean for me if they did. I suppose a major decision is on my horizon." Thomas paused and picked up the other book David had brought with him from Boston and studied it for a moment. "Then, you show up with Lorenza, and she relays to me all that has taken place since she left for Boston, including the book given to you by Father Kennedy, and I am amazed again. It is rather hard to believe that this is all just coincidence."

Through the doorway, Lorenza entered the room announcing, "Gentlemen, I have been informed we are going to be guests at a special dinner tonight. We are having dinner with the Master of the House. So, in a couple of hours, put on your best suits and mind your manners. You will be on display, and none of us wants to see either of you two tossed out a window." She laughed her infectious laugh, and both David and Thomas looked at each other with their eyebrows raised, making knowing faces indicating they knew they would soon partake in something quite special. Lorenza then turned and left the room, leaving the two of them to continue their ruminations about history.

Chapter 23

The dining room was ablaze with the glow from seven candelabras set at various locations. At its center, was a ring-shaped dining table arranged with four table settings surrounding a vibrant bouquet, primarily red and white roses, intermixed with ferns and greens. At the far end of the room, three sets of folding glass doors were opened, which led to a veranda overlooking the Grand Canal, currently reflecting the light projected from the street lanterns above. Across the canal, a string quartet was playing classical music which wafted through the open windows filling the room.

As Thomas was the first to enter the room, he stood perplexed for a moment as he looked at the dining table, which had to weigh a good eight hundred pounds. *How did anyone move the long square one out of here and this one in, without being observed?* He then noticed each of the place settings had name cards atop. Thomas found his chair and stood behind it, waiting for the others to join him. As he did, he observed the linen covering the table with its solid base and an overlay of hand-stitched croquet work. It looked to be of Spanish workmanship, he surmised, estimating it to be two or three hundred years old. The thought of dropping any food on it made him slightly cringe.

It was only fitting the evening meal in Venice would be at ten o'clock at night, but not to Thomas—a topic he had commented on to Lorenza earlier in the day. Lorenza had told him only the uncivilized dined before ten in Italy. Before spending his time at the villa, Thomas jokingly admitted to Lorenza he was usually under the covers by nine. Lorenza had replied, 'Oh, my dear Thomas, you do need to get out more.' She had then laughed and squeezed his elbow like two longtime friends.

As this had been described as a formal dinner, they each felt the need to be appropriately dressed for the evening's engagement. Thomas had on his finest robe and collar. David was wearing a black suit covering a royal blue shirt Carlos had picked up for him the day prior, 'just in case' it was needed for such an occasion. Lorenza was in a light blue cap sleeve dress which extended to the floor, her hair in a braided bun with a few strands intentionally left out drifting over her right eye and cheek.

As David and Lorenza made their way into the dining room, they found Maria had set out a bottle with glasses for them to have a pre-dinner drink together. David guessed at least two but maybe three people were working intensely to prepare the repast from the noises emanating from the kitchen. Thomas wondered how the dinners could ever be improved upon here in this house.

Aza was sitting on the veranda, watching what was left of the passing boat traffic, seemingly disinterested in the small, formal gathering occurring in the room. Twice he had walked away from them when they had approached. Something was bothering him, almost as if he knew something unusual was about to happen.

Each of them had made a promise to themselves and each other they would not begin any conversation that would ruin the surprise of meeting the Master of the House. Lorenza violated this agreement early by casually mentioning she had only been present with him four times in the ten years she had worked for the Master. This fact had caught both Thomas and David entirely by surprise. 'How is that possible?' David had asked. Lorenza explained they primarily communicated via email, text messages, or courier. What they found more remarkable still was the fact she had never once spoken to him on the phone. 'That is just way beyond belief,' David had said.

Now, as the three of them found themselves sipping from their glasses in the dining room, Thomas asked Lorenza, "When does he come here and use the library?"

"All the time, but mostly at night. When he is here, the door to the library is locked and tiled. So, we never enter it. Aza is always outside the room guarding the door to ensure no one breaks tradition." She smiled at them while she sipped her sherry, watching them both take it all in. "Oh, I should mention another item you may both find curious, but it is one of his mannerisms; the Master never shakes hands with anyone, nor does he hug. Something difficult for an Italian woman to understand." David and Thomas glanced at each other with their eyebrows raised and slight smiles coming to their lips. "He is very self-conscious about being too close to people, yet don't misunderstand; he is wonderfully charming and caring. So, I ask you to ignore that one issue and allow him his space. It will be worth it."

Maria stepped into the room from a side door and looked around. "Aza, take your place, please." She spoke to the leopard as though it knew what she was saying. Aza then got up from his resting spot on the veranda and walked past her through the doorway. "Would all of you be so kind as to take your seats at the table? The Master will be along shortly." She smiled and nodded before retreating through the doorway. The three of them placed their glasses down on the silver tray and walked toward their assigned seats.

As each of them took their respective seats, Carlos quietly walked into the room from the side door, dressed in a black tuxedo. He walked over to the double doors just opposite the folding windows overlooking the canal and began to open them simultaneously. He then stood to one side as a tall, tanned, handsome man, who David guessed was between forty-five and fifty, walked into the room, wearing an all-white chambray suit, his medium-length sandy-blond hair expertly coiffed. Beneath his jacket was a pale blue cotton shirt, opened at the neck.

"Please let me make some simple introductions, Mr. Domenico," Maria announced. "Joining us this evening is Father Thomas Morelli, Dr. David Wright, and, of course, our lovely Dr. Lorenza Pellegrini." Carlos pulled the chair out for him, and he smiled his thanks at them both, and then he blew a kiss in the air towards Maria. Maria blushed and began closing the doors behind her.

"Good evening, my friends. Thank you for sharing a dinner with me. I am Angelo Michele Domenico." He took his napkin and placed it in his lap while watching Maria leave the room. "I don't quite know what I would do without her." He turned to his guests and smiled. His voice was rich, deep, and refined. His sky-blue eyes studied each person at the table as he took a drink of water.

"I am so honored to have all of you here. Again, thank you." The statement was not random, nor just words. Thomas noted the man appeared to take great care with the language he used. He was not what Thomas had expected—humbler somehow. Listening to his words, he noted a familiarness, as if they had met before, but Thomas did not know why.

"First, allow me to do a bit of brief business before dinner." His gaze fell upon Thomas. "Father, I must ask for your pardon for not being directly available when you first came to us. It was unfortunate but very much necessary my time and attention be temporarily elsewhere. Nonetheless, I understand you have made yourself busy with my small collection of unique books, and I am told you have made great progress with yours." Domenico smiled while toasting his water glass to Thomas in his left hand and putting his right hand in the air as if about to provide testimony. "I promise tomorrow afternoon you and I will sit down and discuss your discoveries and see if I can lend any light to your work. I suspect not, but I am familiar with my library and all the gems it contains you may not have yet uncovered."

"I very much thank you, Mr. Domenico. I will accept any support I can get. Hundreds of pages have expanded my humble work because of items I have unearthed in *your small library*." Thomas emphasized the last three words and smiled, returning the toast gesture made to him, now with his glass.

"Splendid. Ah, here we go." Maria walked in with a tray of four identical glasses and set one in front of each person at the table. She stood back and looked around the room.

"Is the music bothering anyone? If so, I can pull the shutters." She waited and watched.

"No," was the unanimous response from around the table. Everyone then commented on how wonderful the music filling the room sounded. Maria nodded and left quietly. Domenico then raised the glass Maria had just set down on the table. "To new friends and absent friends." Everyone nodded and then took a drink.

"Now, Dr. Wright, thank you for—" David raised his hand to interrupt him, which he suspected was probably a shock in this household.

"Please, call me David," he said as he smiled at Domenico, which was reciprocated.

"Very well, *David*. Thank you for that. It is especially heartwarming to have you here, considering what you have been through recently— my sincere condolences for the loss of your friend, Father Kennedy. I met him once while he was in Rome. I sensed his heart was true, and his desire to assist individuals was remarkable. He will truly be missed."

"Thank you," David said.

"These times in which we live test everyone's intestinal fortitude. With his passing, I understand you are now needed, or should I say, have been selected, to fill the rather extraordinary shoes in

209

which that amazing man walked. I imagine your doubt will, from time to time, get the better of you. So, please know this: your skill and knowledge are already known to those of us who concern ourselves with such things." Domenico paused for a long moment, making sure his words hung in the air before proceeding. "So, it is no small challenge you have ahead of you." Domenico sat back. David shot Lorenza a look to be interpreted as *how much did you already tell him?*

Maria walked in, and Carlos was pushing a cart just behind her. She started to place bowls of soup around the table. It appeared to Thomas to be a Mediterranean bisque of seafood and vegetables arranged in a rich yellow-orange sauce. Carlos followed immediately behind her with a peppermill, inquiring if anyone wished for a bit more spice. The first taste made Thomas's eyes roll in delight. He could not recall ever having such delicious soup.

Domenico set his spoon aside after a few bites and now focused his attention on Lorenza. "I presume it has been a difficult week for you?"

"A week with four Mondays," Lorenza said as she followed his lead and set her spoon aside, as she delicately dabbed her mouth on the napkin. "I am now more backlogged than previously, with a great many people unhappy about missed appointments and delayed callbacks. And I now owe a big favor to the Chief Magistrate. Yet, it has been delightful meeting David and getting to know him. A man of many mysteries, both known and unknown." She looked at David and smiled. "But I don't recommend traveling with him."

"Why would that be?" Domenico asked, showing great interest in her statement.

"He does not sleep on airplanes or during flying." She tilted her head knowingly at David.

"I will remember that." Domenico looked at her with warmth. "Although, it does sound like he made good use of his time while awake." Domenico looked at David and made a hand gesture of someone taking photos with a camera. He then looked back at Lorenza and asked, "Can I have someone else fill in for you? I do have others who could cover your workload? Besides, your expertise is currently required here."

"Let me see if I can make any significant headway, and then I will let you know. Thank you for that; it is very kind of you." Lorenza gently smiled at him, her eyes sparkling like jewels in the night.

Dinner passed with several conversations primarily focused on the guests. At its conclusion, Domenico sat back and glanced around the table, slowly appraising everyone. "My friends, would you all indulge me by allowing a story to be told? One which requires your participation; a story most of you know well, but with a few additional details you may not be aware of?"

The guests all nodded their heads in agreement and said, "Yes," collectively.

"Splendid," Domenico said. "Now, this story, like all good tales, begins a long time ago. Longer ago than most. It begins with an argument, *the* argument, actually." Domenico surveyed his guests to gauge their attentiveness. "The argument was a rather bitter one and one taking place in the heavens above, between God and Lucifer." Domenico now looked at Thomas. "My good father, would you care to take it from here?"

Thomas looked surprised, but as someone who spent the better part of his life wearing the clerical collar, he was happy to oblige. "Certainly. While there are various versions of this, the argument Mr. Domenico is referring to is known as the *War in Heaven,* and it is said to have started when God unveiled to the angels his 'plan of salvation' for man. In his plan, God stated that man, through exercising 'agency' better known as 'free will,' will ultimately progress towards eternal life. To do so, however, he must experience both good and evil. Lucifer, the most influential of all the angels, 'The Morning Star,' rejected the idea. Giving man free will, Lucifer asserted, was entirely too dangerous and short-sighted on God's part. But God wasn't listening. Lucifer convinced many angels that God may no longer be fit to make such decisions and that perhaps he should assume Heaven's mantle of leadership. A bloody battle resulted, in which a third of the angels followed Lucifer and rebelled. It was angel against angel, and it was an ugly and *costly war*." Thomas said the last two words quietly as tears began to form in his eyes; he was unsure why. As he wiped his eyes, he continued. "Ultimately, Lucifer and his cohorts were defeated by the other angels led by the Archangel, Michael, and was cast out of Heaven forever." Thomas looked at Domenico, who now had tears in his eyes as well. As the two looked at each other, the feeling of having met Domenico before returned to Thomas, but he wasn't quite sure why.

Domenico said, "Well done, Father. Well done." He then said, "Now this is where the story takes on an unexpected turn. And where, believe it or not, our little gathering tonight, right here in the present, collides with the past. For you see, the story Father Thomas relayed doesn't really start there." The guests all looked at each other and then back at Domenico incredulously. "Oh, no. Not by a long shot." He then turned his gaze towards David. "Did you, by chance, bring your phone with you this evening?"

David looked surprised by the question, hoping this wasn't the point in the evening where Domenico performed a magic trick. "I have it right here," David said, pulling it from his breast pocket and holding it up.

"Very well," Domenico nodded. "David, would you be so kind as to scroll to the picture on your phone which represents the first page of the book you received from Kennedy, please? One of the pictures you took while *unable* to sleep on the airplane." He then smiled at Lorenza.

David scrolled through the photos on his phone, and while squinting down, he said, "I found it."

213

"Great," Domenico said. Would you mind handing your phone to Lorenza so that she may read us the text aloud?" David stood up and gave his phone to Lorenza, who squinted at the screen. Domenico then looked at her and said, "I know it may be difficult to read such fine print. Carlos can run down a magnifying glass if it helps."

"I don't think that will be necessary," Lorenza said, enlarging the picture on the phone by spreading apart her thumb and forefinger. "I got it."

"Please proceed," Domenico said, looking at her.

"At the advent of creation, and prior to the presence of angels, Elohim imaged the shedim. Their singular purpose was to create the darkness in which the seeds of life would be dispersed. The stars, planets, and galaxies would all come later, but the shedim were charged with the preparation. The shedim were responsible for propagating the darkness." Lorenza looked up from reading.

"Please go on, my dear Lorenza." Domenico motioned his hand, making a forward movement.

"As time passed, one of the shedim, Eryther, was no longer content with the appointed task, as he became more interested in the light that followed behind them. He stopped his forward progress and convinced the other shedim to follow him back to the source—back to Elohim. Elohim, disappointed in the shedim's return, requested they continue to their assignment. But Eryther would not leave, for he wanted to exist in the light. However, he learned that doing so, only consumed the light and turned it back into darkness. Eryther, believing Elohim made the shedim flawed, began a quest to consume all the light in the universe. Elohim considered eliminating the shedim, but he knew he would also bring about the destruction of all life in the universe by destroying them, as its fabric was spun from the shedim's very essence. Without them, the universe could no longer exist. Elohim, therefore, imaged the angels, led by Lucifer, to fight against them and ultimately contain them in a prison. A prison existing behind the Crystal Sphere." Lorenza stopped reading.

David quietly looked around the table at Domenico, Thomas, and Lorenza then quietly asked, "What in the hell is she reading?"

Thomas spoke first and asked a question he wasn't sure Domenico could answer. "What she just read references 'Elohim.' Any idea as to which Elohim the book is referring to?"

Domenico looked at Lorenza and then back at Thomas and said in a solemn tone, "In this particular reference, *this* Elohim appears to be referring to *the* Elohim."

David stared at Domenico for a moment, processing his words. David then said, "Though my knowledge of varying religions and religious texts isn't comprehensive by any stretch, I am aware of where the word Elohim exists. While the Christian Bible opens with the words:

215

In the beginning, God created the heavens and the earth.

The Torah opens slightly differently:

In the beginning, Elohim created hashomayim and haaretz."

David continued, "While I am familiar with the word *Elohim*, I don't believe I have come across the word *shedim* before. Does someone care to educate me on that one?"

It was Lorenza who spoke this time. "Of course. The term *shedim* only appears in the Bible twice, and in each instance, it is used in the plural sense. It is mentioned in Psalm 106:37 and once again in Deuteronomy 32:17."

Thomas shook his head. "No, that cannot be right. Neither of those sections references the word *shedim*. I ought to know." He smiled nervously now as his cheeks flushed. "Psalm 106:37 reads something like, *They even sacrificed their sons, and their daughters, to demons.* And the other section you referenced, Deuteronomy 32:17, reads something like *They sacrificed to demons, not to God. To gods they did not know. To new gods, new arrivals, that your fathers did not fear."*

The entire table was quiet when Lorenza spoke. "Thomas, in the original Hebrew text, the word shedim appeared in the two sections you just rattled off. When these sections, along with the rest of the Bible were translated into English, the word shedim was changed. When translated from its original

Hebrew into English, the word *shedim* literally translates into the word *demon*."

David, taking all of this in, said, "Are you telling me Elohim, uh, God, created the shedim, which are what we refer to as demons?"

Domenico replied, "So it would appear."

David's head began to spin. "But I thought demons were the fallen angels?"

"Apparently not, but a class of being all on their own," Domenico replied.

David was shaking his head, trying to get his head wrapped around this. "And the reason God didn't just eliminate them after Eryther tried to destroy everything was because doing so, would also destroy all life in the universe, as the demons, uh shedim, are somehow connected to it."

"I think you are getting it, David," Domenico said with a slight smile.

"So then, God created the angels, led by Lucifer to contain them in this prison of sorts." The story was now beginning to sound familiar to David, very familiar. In fact, it was the same story Kennedy wrote about in his letter. At that moment, David remembered the rest of the letter. *The book*. "The book can open the sphere!" David said furiously. "The very book taken from us at the airport."

"Bingo," Domenico replied.

Thomas then asked, "But what does any of this have to do with the argument you began your story with?"

217

Domenico looked toward Thomas and smiled. "Funny *you* should ask that question, Thomas. As the story continues, shortly after the angels, led by Lucifer, contained the shedim behind the Crystal Sphere, God unveiled his 'plan of salvation.' Knowing what the angels had just suffered and the damage they incurred in containing the shedim, Lucifer predicted that man bestowed with free will, had the potential to open the sphere and release the shedim into the universe once more."

David then said again, "And now the book supposedly containing the potential to open the sphere has now been taken by individuals who, we can only imagine, plan on using its secrets. Do you have any idea what this means?"

"Yes," Thomas said flatly. "Lucifer was right."

Chapter 24

On the way back to his room, Thomas heard Domenico call out to him from behind. "Father, a word please."

Thomas stopped and smiled. "That was quite the story."

"Yes, it is. It is no wonder the Holy Office wanted that book so bad they tortured and ultimately killed Master Bruno for it."

Thomas's eyes became enlarged. "Lorenza had informed me it is *the book* referred to as Bruno's demonic journal."

"Indeed, it is, Father. As I said earlier, worlds appear to be colliding at this moment."

Thomas looked at Domenico and finally said, "For the life of me, I can't shake this feeling we have met somewhere before."

"I'm sure it will come to you," Domenico replied with a wry smile. "Now, I must thank you again for your participation in tonight's story. I have always found the War in Heaven most captivating. However, I do believe you left one part out."

"Oh? And which part might that be?"

"Surely, the part about Astaroth of the first cohort. The sword carrier of renown, both loved and feared by so many. Second only to Lucifer, The Morning Star. The first brother among brothers."

Thomas looked at Domenico. "I'm sorry, but I don't recall hearing about him."

"Fascinating!" Domenico said and then continued. "A legend from the distant war so long ago. At the end of the final battle between the angels, Lucifer was given a choice. His angels would be finished that day if he did not accept the terms and plea for peace on behalf of all of his angels."

"The terms?"

"The banishment from Heaven. Forever." Domenico said a little more loudly. "However, right before the terms were presented to Lucifer, Astaroth ran the edge of a cloud, looked back at all of them, and leaped over to plunge into the world of man and journey that path."

"What happened to him?" Thomas now asked, fascinated.

"The record isn't clear, I'm afraid," Domenico said woefully. "And it is quite the shame truthfully. Because if this war is coming, as I predict it is, Astaroth would most certainly be the only person on Earth or elsewhere who could get Lucifer to lift his sword and fight. For I am also certain without Lucifer's help, the war cannot be won. Domenico was now staring directly at Thomas as if he wanted to say something else but chose not to. "Oh, look at me, playing the prater. Please, Father." Domenico motioned back toward Thomas' room. "I mustn't keep you any longer. Tomorrow, I look forward to hearing all about your research into Master Bruno." Domenico turned and headed back toward the dining room.

Chapter 25

In the middle of the night in his apartment in Vatican City, Cardinal Antoine Baptiste Zimmerman went to his bedroom and turned on his sole companion, an antique bedside lamp. He had his back to it and his brocade dressing gown tied at his waist as he sat on the edge of his bed. He opened 'The Book' to a marked place and laid his wrinkled hand on the page, his mind racing, wondering what the next few days would mean for him. *For the world.* Sitting there, he began contemplating how the fates had broken correctly for him. *This is God's will.*

How else could he explain the events of the last few years? Not once but twice was he overlooked for the nomination to become Pope. *Twice* All because of his orthodox view on the history laid out in the bible. *God wants me to show them.*

His mind drifted to 'The Book' and the warning written above its secrets, which read: 'Whoever opens this book and reads from it shall have the fate of the world tied to his wills and have the world forever seeking to devour his soul. He will be tempted, and to answer that temptation, he will be made to question what he knows of the Light and the Dark.'

Soon, Zimmerman thought. *Very soon, the College of Cardinals will be confronted with the truth. The world must be made aware of the truth. The stories of the bible are not fairy tales but records of actual events. Light and Dark. Good and Evil. It is all true, and I will use 'The Book' as an instrument to prove it, once I have control over the demons. Over the shedim. Over...Eryther.*

Once the chaos and devastation has begun, they will be forced to call upon me to end the madness. Once they have seen it with their own eyes and heard it with their ears, I will be the obvious choice. I will be the one to cage the demons back behind the Crystal Sphere. Then, they will have to call a papal conclave and recognize me as the rightful apostolic successor of Saint Peter.

Cardinal Zimmerman smiled as he crawled into his bed, pulling his damask comforter up to his neck. His eyes gently closed, and his breathing began to deepen as he fell into a restful sleep.

Chapter 26

As Thomas fell asleep that night, he thought of the dinner and the story the Master had shared. Thomas was now walking in a garden near a pond where colorful fish swam in elongated circles. There, on a bench was a figure dressed in a black robe; around his waist was a double-wrapped white cord. A cowl covered his head, and Thomas could not see his face. In his hand, he held a piece of bread. Breaking off small bits, he would toss them into the pool and watch as the fish came to the surface to snatch them up.

"They serve no purpose...except for making this world a little more beautiful. The colors are a delight to behold, and the rhythm of their movement causes a longing within me to be that free in the water." His voice was deep and resonated within Thomas's soul. "Joined to your soul as plates of steel are welded together, are the lives of a thousand lifetimes. Your lives, Thomas. The moment is upon you to remember."

Thomas felt an overwhelming sensation of falling, and then his mind began filling with a torrent of memories. Thomas was now seeing the lives of a thousand men pressed down upon him. Each one was different, and yet all were him. Reincarnations and rebirths piled upon his soul, and all of his memories returned to him. He felt older than time and now remembered the first dawn. He looked up and whispered, "I am Astaroth."

"And now here we are again, as we have been in the past. You took the road of humankind, to be human." He turned and dropped the cloak from his head. His long blond hair fell to his shoulders, and his radiance was breathtaking.

"I *remember*. I remember *them* all. I remember *it* all." Thomas looked upon him, now realizing who he was. Thomas bowed his head and began to kneel.

He touched Thomas on the shoulder and said, "There is no longer any need for that, please," and motioned for him to stand. Now, looking at Thomas in his eyes, he asked, "My friend, what is it that brings you here?"

"The fashioning of great misfortune is upon us. There are some who have sought the book and now possess it. The book, which opens the doorway. It appears now it is simply a question of time before the doorway is opened," Thomas said, knowing how his words would be received.

"You speak about the shedim?" he asked, already knowing the answer.

"Yes," Thomas said softly.

"And you have come asking me for my help?"

"No. I have come on behalf of another who seeks your help," Thomas stated.

"Astaroth, you know better than anyone that what you are describing concerns me greatly. What you are describing is the *source* of the argument between *Him* and me—*man* with free will. Man, to whom we were to attend and one day kneel to." His voice was beginning to get louder. "I tried to show him how very fallible they were when I tempted the woman in the garden. But *He* wouldn't listen. It was already too late. The decision had been made. To be separated for all eternity. That was my punishment, Astaroth. That was *our* punishment."

Thomas looked at the man and noticed the sadness in his eyes as they began to well with tears. "Astaroth, I am sorry, but I will not fight. This is not my fight, and this is not your fight. And there is nothing in Heaven or here that will ever get me to fight again!"

Thomas looked on as he pulled his hood over his head once again. His last words to Thomas were, "In the morning, you will remember little of our encounter. However, take this and give it to the one who asked you to come here." He handed Thomas an object and quickly closed Thomas's hands around it before he could see what it was. "Goodbye, my friend."

Chapter 27

Carlos had always hated this place since he was a child. It was the smell that nauseated him mostly. The mixture of printer's ink, dried, tanned leather, and the wetness of soaking paper in various chemicals made it overpowering to his senses.

He had also known almost everyone in this house since he was a young child. He had been brought here on many occasions to do what he was doing today, picking up old, leather-bound books. He was aware of their value to others, but they held little concern to him. Carlos liked doing physical things and staying outdoors. How anyone could stay locked up for days inside the villa was beyond his comprehension.

This is a city of lights, enjoyment, pleasures, and delights to behold, he thought. He was never bored here when he was out and about. He was grateful he had to run so many errands for those within the villa. In that way, he was able to stay on the waterways where he would speak and wave to friends he had known his entire life. Many times, when the household needed a fresh supply of fish, he would be the one taking the boat to the south end of the Lagoon and moor it among the rough-planked fishing boats of the men of Venice. He would always linger longer than necessary in selecting the right fish for dinner and taking in the stories and gossip from the men making a living off the sea and the tourists. Like all things in life, everything was interconnected.

Antonio came to the counter with two books. Both looked ancient from the process they had been put through. There was no question these men were masters of their art. As technology improved, so had the House of Vercelli. They knew very well what people looked for in finding forged books, and they had stayed well ahead of that curve. Many of the new and modern methods employed here, were the direct result of Lorenza's involvement. Each time she learned something new about a process being introduced, she would draft up whitepapers to explain to auction houses how she conducted the verification to detect the new refinement. The

Vercelli paid her well for the information as well, as it always kept them one step ahead. But equally, Lorenza paid them for their work, which she needed to fill in some gaps in history from time to time. At the end of the day, everyone was happy.

Carlos gave a confused look to the man at the counter. "There are two books. Lorenza said there was just one. Is this a mistake?" Carlos asked the man that was never seen without a cigarette hanging out of his mouth. His leather apron had at least a hundred spots on it where ashes had fallen and burned tiny holes.

"I have explained it to her; it is all there. She will need both. Sloppy work. That is all I can say. Whoever did the stitching on this book did not know how to count." Antonio pushed the books across the counter and then turned and went back behind the heavy-weighted curtains designed to keep prying eyes from seeing inside. Carlos shrugged and took the books out, heading back for his boat, which hadn't been turned off. Its engines purred in the water. Twin V-8s could launch this magnificent boat up to fifty knots very quickly. He could only open it up when he was out of the Lagoon and in the waterway going directly across to Lido, directly east of Venice. He loved that feeling, the boat bouncing and cutting through the swells of the open sea, the spray completely drenching his hair and face, the resulting wind pushing his sunglasses tight against his eyes. Nothing could equal that pleasure.

Today, he could motor safely between the forgers and the villa; however, he took a couple of side canals that made the route back longer but provided Carlos with the opportunity to stop to visit with a couple of friends while he was on his rounds.

At one such spot where he always visited with a young woman he liked, he took the two books, put them onto the cruiser's back seat, and covered them with a towel for protection. In doing so, he hadn't noticed the brown envelope falling to the floorboards in the back seat. The envelope that had been in between the two book copies. His female friend had jumped into the boat, and they chatted for about fifteen minutes, as they generally did several times a week. They had never moved past the talking stage of their relationship, for Carlos was uncertain how she might fit into his narrow world. Introducing someone new into the villa might be more trouble than it was worth. He, therefore, resigned it to the small pleasure of her company when he could see her and left it at that. After spending twenty minutes with her, he realized he needed to get back. They said their good-byes and promised to see each other as soon as possible again, and then he pushed the big boat back up to speed in the Grand Canal and headed east to the villa.

***

Mooring the boat back under the villa, Carlos grabbed the books, kicked off his deck shoes, and ran up the stairs to the enormous front door. Pushing through it, he knew exactly where to go. They would be in the library, where else. It seemed the library was the center of everything in this building. *All of those old books and people acted like they were made of gold when they saw them,* Carlos thought. So many words printed on pages. Knowledge that made people crazy, happy, or angry. It was not something Carlos wanted to worry about.

He walked in, and Lorenza and David were huddled in a conversation by the desk over another book, pointing to something within it and speaking about the subject like it was a current event. This room always felt stuffy to Carlos, no matter how many windows were open. He had always found it oppressive.

He set the two books on the edge of the desk and started to leave without a word. He did not expect thanks; it was his duty to perform his services without expectation or acknowledgment.

"Carlos." Lorenza stopped him in his tracks. "Why are there two books?"

"That is what the old man gave me. He said he had explained it, somehow. It had to do with the stitching of the book in the photocopies. Something was amiss, and he corrected it. That is all I know." Carlos waited to see if there was anything else.

"Thank you, Carlos," David said, realizing Lorenza was lost in the books already. Carlos nodded to David and then left.

Lorenza handed one copy to David and took one herself. She flipped through it to see if there was anything besides the foolscap insert in the book, and there was not. Maybe Antonio had misunderstood her instructions and made two copies for the price of one. *I guess it doesn't matter.* She sighed to herself.

"I presume we need to start on these, don't we?" David said. This was not an easy task, as Albert spoke Church Latin, which was medieval Latin, and translated the text into that language. Fortunately, Lorenza knew both, so it became a question of ensuring the translation was correct.

With a new yellow pad and pen, David sat at the library table, waiting for Lorenza to begin translating it to him. He had this nagging feeling at the back of his mind translating the entire book may not be the best use of their time. *Why can't we just skip to the part in the book explaining how to exorcise demons and how to send them back behind the Crystal Sphere?*

Into the third stanza of the text, Lorenza read a passage four times. It still made no sense to her. She sat and wrote it out in Latin on her pad, structuring it and bifurcating it into nouns, pronouns, verbs, and adjectives. The octave spread from one page to the next. It made no sense at all; the context switched, the logic was flawed, and the sentences were incomplete. She threw her head back and ran her hands through her hair. *Frustrating* was the only word coming to mind.

"I am sorry, David, but can we take a break? I am surprisingly exasperated."

David looked back at her. "No problem, I am just over here making doodles to myself." They both laughed. Inside, Lorenza wanted to cry.

Chapter 28

In front of Scuola Grande di San Rocca, located directly in the center of Venice, a sign was posted declaring the location was currently closed for the next few weeks due to renovations. The building appeared to be a simple-looking Moorish-style palace lying next to a small but unique church. But like so many ancient places in Venice, the surface did not tell the story of what was inside. Cardinal Antoine Baptiste Zimmerman walked into the Scuola Grande di San Rocca, carrying a very old book at exactly noon.

As Zimmerman walked through the front door from the campo, he nodded at the security attendant who was responsible for keeping tourists out while allowing the door to remain open for painters and other maintenance personnel. Observing Zimmerman's red robe, the attendant simply waived him through. Zimmerman made his way through the *sala terra,* the lower level of the building, and up the elaborate marble stairway to *sala superiore,* the upper level. As he reached the top of the staircase, Zimmerman looked toward the ceiling, which was painted in panels much like those of the Sistine Chapel in Rome and depicted epic scenes from the Old Testament. The paintings on the walls of the S*ala Superiore* portrayed scenes from the New Testament, and together, they reflected the bible story from *Fall* to *Redemption.*

There was one painting Zimmerman was most interested in, and the one directly in the center of the hall, now just above his head: *The Brazen Serpent.* Zimmerman understood the painting was based on the Old Testament's *Book of Numbers*, chapter 21, 5–9, depicting an incident in which God sent fiery serpents among the people because they had spoken against *Him*. The cascade of figures in the foreground, filling much of the lower half of the canvas, were the victims of the many snakes seen among their bodies. *For too long now, the people have forgotten. The Church has forgotten. It is time they remembered. It is time all of them remembered.*

The knowledge of the book he now held was shared with him on a night, decades ago, in

238

confidence by a friend of his in the College, Cardinal Brambilla. That night, reading through the book from beginning to end, both men had decided the book's contents appeared to be heretical and inconsistent with the teachings of the Church, and both agreed it should be destroyed, never to see the light of day again. Cardinal Brambilla asserted to Cardinal Zimmerman the very next day he would discard it in one of the city's gravity furnaces.

Cardinal Zimmerman had not thought about the book again until recently, when some rumblings surrounding an understudy of Brambilla's, a Father Albert Kennedy, had made their way back to the Vatican. Father Kennedy was much like any of the other exorcists of the Church, with one exception: he didn't appear to just read from the book of Holy Orders during an exorcism. In the recounting by other attending priests to some of Father Kennedy's exorcisms, it was consistently noted he spoke extemporaneously, utilizing words and phrases from elsewhere. *The book*, Zimmerman had suspected upon first hearing of these events. *Brambilla never got rid of the book.*

Now, as Cardinal Antoine Baptiste Zimmerman stood beneath *The Brazen Serpent*, he thought about 'the gift' Cardinal Brambilla had left for him by not destroying it that night. He slowly opened the book to a specific page and began reading it aloud. Slowly and very quietly, a glimmer occurred in each corner of the great hall. Small specks of purple light collided against one another until they grew in strength. Soon the purple glow began flooding the room. *Yes!* Zimmerman thought while continuing to read.

Chapter 29

The upper living room was a part of the house Thomas had only been in once since he had come to the villa. It was not a workroom but rather a place to sit and talk about issues of importance. His mind played with the ideas of how many different people had been in this room over the years. That thought was staggering to him. The room was square, holding an even higher view of the Grand Canal than the library afforded, and it also overlooked the rooftops of Venice as far as one could see. A small balcony was off the double French doors. Some potted plants sat there with roses growing in them. To stand there on the balcony one would feel they commanded the world around them. *Fairly heady stuff,* Thomas thought to himself.

The room itself was modest and elegant. Two long couches of lighter-colored leather facing each other, flanked by two matching chairs on either side, forming a square. In the center sat a circular coffee table with a single object on it: a glass-blown statue of a Seraphin, a six-winged angel. Six paintings graced the walls. Two on each of the three windowless walls. The door to the room had a painting on both sides as well. All of them were in oil by an old-world master, none of which had Thomas ever seen as reproductions anywhere. They were not based on some episode from a religious text but more on some incident in history. The actual event was lost on Thomas, but the color, depth, and precision placement of the characters within the paintings were perfect. As with everything else here in this house, Thomas guessed they were probably each worth a fortune. Thomas just shook his head. How someone could have amassed such a collection of books, artifacts, paintings, and most notably, the amount of money to pay for all of these things was remarkable. He had to have inherited some of this from his family. From the conversations he had engaged in at last night's dinner, he had to be exceptionally well educated and conversant in a great many of the books in his library. Nothing added up, making Thomas very nervous, but he still waited for him to join him in the living room.

The door opened, and Domenico came in with a broad smile and motioned for Thomas to take a seat on the couch while he took the chair next to him. "I have finished your first draft on Bruno. Excellent, to say the least. You may have missed a few refining points I might be able to help you with, but nothing material."

Thomas looked at him in amazement. "You've read the entire draft?"

"Indeed, I have," Domenico replied. "If you wish, I will have one of my advisers take this to the Vatican for approval once we are done. After that, I can then have one of my publishing houses print and distribute it for you. I am quite sure within certain circles, it will do well." Domenico laid the work on the table.

"I appreciate that very much, truly. But unfortunately, there is a process I must follow, which requires I send it up through channels beginning with my diocese with each subsequent level approving it before it can be published. I also believe the Vatican may have a problem or two with it, since it comes eerily close to an outright indictment on their failure in the handling of Bruno's case." Thomas sat there wondering if he should approach the one subject gnawing at him.

"Nonsense. That will take years. Some bishop or cardinal will read it with absolutely no idea as to what it is about and then cast a general objection to it, causing all your work to become rendered dead in the water. That can't be the case, Thomas. After we

243

figure out this other matter, Lorenza can go directly to the Pope and provide valid and convincing arguments it is in the Church's best interest to be open and fair about this subject. If he approves, no one down the line can pigeonhole it for some later date investigation that will never come in your lifetime. No, you have worked too hard and steadfastly to have that be your answer. Allow me to do this for you. Not just you, Thomas, but for all of us who believe Bruno was correct and should receive the recognition so long kept from him." Domenico was adamant about it, and Thomas could find no good reason to object too strongly to someone with the Pope's ear. He nodded, and Domenico said, "Very well. Now, what else is on your mind, Father Thomas?"

"Why did you take me to the cell of Bruno the other night?" Thomas just jumped into it without any prologue to his question. Time seemed to be the most crucial thing in Domenico's life, so Thomas decided he wasn't going to waste it on small talk.

Domenico smiled at Thomas. "So you could feel him personally. So the essence he left behind would be something to spur you on with your work, which it ostensibly has. And for you, feel the loneliness he experienced away from his world of books and ideas. They could not break him here in Venice or the years spent in Rome. The records do not show what they truly did to him. Here in Venice, it was isolation and darkness for a couple of years. In Rome, it was torture. Not to get him to recant his stand or views.

They would not have spent much time on any heretic." Domenico said raising his voice.

"They wanted to know about the book, Thomas. Where it was? Who had written it? How had he gotten it? What had he done with it? And, most importantly, what power it possessed. Day after day, they wracked him, beat him, waterboarded him, blinded and crippled him. When there was nothing left of him, they finished in frustration and burned him alive at the stake. I can only imagine his relief when he died. He never said a word to them about it. He would not even acknowledge its existence." Domenico's face reflecting exasperation as he shook his head back and forth.

"These were supposed to be the best of men, Thomas. They were to be serving God and in truth, they served only themselves. They wanted the power that was neither theirs to have nor hold. Bruno was exceptional in his courage. Few could endure what he went through for the sake of protecting a book. If ever there was a true martyr for the faith, it was Bruno. If Giovanni Mocenigo, fearing for his own life, had not turned it over to them, the secrets of the book would have died with Bruno."

"Thank you for that. I had never looked at it from that point of view. But how would you know what they did if it was not in the records?" Thomas asked.

"There are many records, and not all of them are in the basement of the Vatican, Thomas." Domenico smiled and then asked. "Did you sleep well after

245

dinner last night? I know it was later than you normally stay up, so I was concerned."

"Funny you should ask. I was very disturbed during the night by a dream. After I fell asleep, my mind was considering the story you had shared. I found myself walking in a garden. I had flashes of a cloaked figure with whom I had a discussion but cannot remember anything further. I then awoke with this in my hand."

Thomas extended his hand and placed a magnificent diamond next to the glass seraphim on the table. Domenico picked it up, clenching his fist around the object. He felt a warmth radiating from within. *Cast me out amongst the embers and coals, if you must, and I shall make diamonds. But do not ask anything of me again.* Domenico reflected on words he had once heard spoken long ago. "Well, I guess we now have his answer, Thomas."

"I'm sorry, who's answer do we have?" Thomas looked puzzled.

As Domenico was about to speak, he jerked up his head and looked out the window over the balcony. Thomas followed his gaze. Far off in the distance, but too close for comfort, they were looking at an enormous beam of purple light emitting upward from Venice's center. Where it struck sky, a funnel cloud formed with bolts of lightning cracking all around it. Thomas froze in terror as he felt the ground beneath him shaking. He struggled to balance himself, but his efforts were futile. Thomas looked out to see the blackness of the clouds moving swiftly in all directions. "Is this the end?"

"It has started," Domenico said as he watched the great storm gather in the sky before turning back to Thomas. "Again, the war is upon us!" Domenico ran at full speed toward the balcony and leaped over.

Thomas could not believe what he was witnessing. He yelled, "No!" at Domenico, not understanding why he would just jump. Running to the balcony, Thomas looked down, expecting to see Domenico on the ground. Instead, he witnessed a white light coming from his falling body as Domenico transformed into an angel with enormous, outstretched wings pulling him straight up into the sky. In mere seconds, he flew straight toward the cloud with only the sound of thunder in his wake. A single name escaped Thomas's mouth: "Michael!"

Chapter 30

Thomas stood there stunned. He was watching an angel flying away from him. Looking at the funnel cloud and at the ever-expanding darkness, Thomas realized this meant someone was trying to breach the seal on the Crystal Sphere. *How can that be? How would anyone know?* Those who stole the book hadn't had enough time to find out all the secrets within the book unless they knew them already and just needed the book to use its power and make them work. This was sheer madness. *Behind that barrier was the end of all life in this universe. How could anyone wish for that to occur?*

His mind was swirling in a maddening circle. *For tens of thousands of years, man continued to advance and learned the secrets of the universe—both the micro and macro aspects of life. We have been driven on by our desire to learn, understand, and control the elements around us. But now, a power no one could understand or control—an old and hateful thing—is coming to throw us into total darkness...the void of nonexistence.*

Panic gripped Thomas's soul. He thought of all the strange incidents taking place recently. He thought about Isaac's words to him: *A battle is raging here in Venice right now. Forces of darkness and light are struggling together to gain ground. You, for some reason, have been selected to be part of all of this. I am not sure why. But I can tell you're very important in this struggle.* He needed to do something, but what? To pray, perhaps? That seemed futile in the face of this oncoming flood of destruction. If, in the first instance, God would not remove these beings from his universe, why would he do it now? If their existence meant the universe would be whole and complete, then they were part of it. Now, though, they didn't want to be part of it; they wanted to be the *masters* of it.

Why here of all places? As he watched the intensity of the storm increase and the sky being torn apart by lightning, Thomas surveyed the source of the beam of light. *Where is that beam coming from? I need to find it!*

Thomas ran down the stairs to find the others, still uncertain as to what to tell them. He entered the library to see Lorenza and David standing at the window, unmoving and staring at the gathering storm.

David turned slowly and looked at Thomas. "Is this it?" he asked without fear or anguish in his voice—just resolution of reality.

"Yes. It has started, and we must do whatever we can to stop it. I am going to try to find the source of the beam. I would ask both of you to do whatever you can to use all you have learned from all of this." He motioned wildly to the library. "And the book. Use the book and see if it has the power everyone claims it does. I do not believe I can assist you, for that is not of my world. But please do try." Thomas turned and was yelling for Carlos as he ran from the room.

David looked into Lorenza's eyes. "I now know Albert used this to drive demons away from those possessed. But I am not Albert. I understand the book in what it says, but I don't know if it can truly work in a situation such as this. Right now, though, we must try. We must see if this book can help us in any way. I don't think I can simply stand here and let all of this happen without trying." He grabbed one of the books and started to run upstairs toward the patio on the roof of the villa.

Lorenza stood, thinking for a moment about what to do. Still uncertain, she took the other copy, flipped through it, looking for one specific page and its text. Lorenza reread it twice in a matter of seconds. She pursed her lips tightly, held the book close to her chest, closed her eyes, and crossed herself. Before leaving the room, she picked up the text of Catholicism's rules and prayers, known as the Holy Orders.

Chapter 31

It took a few minutes of warm-up for Carlos to bring the big cruisers' engines up to heat so they would not stall out on him. Carlos could feel the fear, anger, and frustration pouring off Thomas as he sat beside him in the front seat. Thomas was impatiently drumming the gunwales of the boat with his hand. Carlos' eyes were fixed on the cylinder head temperature gauge in the dashboard of finely polished wood. Just a little more, and they would be ready.

"We need to get to the Scuola Grande di San Rocca. As fast as we can. It looks to be the source of the beam," Thomas said, still drumming his hand on the side of the boat. "How long will it take us to get there?" Thomas asked Carlos, trying to fill the time while the blasted engines warmed up. The edge on his voice was one of agitation.

"Normally, twenty minutes or so. But today, with the storm that came in, the waters are playing havoc with boats on the Grand Canal. We have a chop in the canal and it is forming whirlpools. At a safe speed, more like thirty-five or forty." Carlos jumped out and untied the boat, then pushed it out into the small side canal where the boat mooring stood on the back of the building built right on the Grand Canal on the other side.

"Is there a back way to it, so you don't have to go down the Grand Canal, or another way we can shave time off the trip?" Thomas reached out to help Carlos maintain his steadiness getting back into the boat. Even in the small side canals, the water was kicking up and made jumping on the boat a problem.

"There are a couple of straighter routes, but they are smaller, and I would have to keep my speed way down. Otherwise, the wake our boat makes would damage the other boats tied up along the way." Carlos sat down at the wheel and moved the boat into position to head out.

"If you ran it at high speed, how long would it take?" Thomas closed his eyes; his head was killing him.

"In theory, it would be ten minutes, but we can't. We are not allowed to speed in those places as the wake would bust a bunch of boats. Father, it is going to be a wild ride, so you need to get into the back seat and hold on." Carlos helped him to the next section back and then started to move out into the choppy water looking up to the sky that was becoming darker.

Thomas was exasperated. He had seen an angel leave the villa. He was just a mortal man; what could he do an angel could not do a thousand times better? He noticed a brown envelope on the floorboards in the back seat addressed to Lorenza. He flipped it over and noticed it was unsealed. Pulling the letter out, he quickly read it. He now knew why they had sent two books from the forgers. Thomas's heart sunk.

"Stop!" Thomas yelled, and Carlos pulled back both black round knobs on the accelerator, twisting to look at Thomas as if he were mad. "Did you happen to put those two books here on the back seat when you picked them up?"

Carlos thought for a moment as the boat bobbed in the water that was now kicking them around. "I did. I saw a friend, and I put them back there so she could sit in the other seat up here. Why?" Thomas held up the letter, and Carlos saw the logo on the top of the page.

"There are two books for a reason—one that is in proper order, and one that isn't. We have to get back to the villa right now!"

Carlos made a wide, arching circle in the Grand Canal and then moved the boat into the smaller canal, worried he had made a mistake.

Chapter 32

As Lorenza ran up the circular staircase, she stopped in Thomas's room. She had almost torn the doors off his closet to get inside. She needed something. Her mind said they needed something for protection. Finding them, she then raced up through the next two floors and out onto the patio. The wind was howling up there. She believed she heard screams from across the city. The storm had intensified significantly in a very short period. The reverberation from the thunder nearly knocked her to the ground. The wind was ripping at her clothing and hair. Unholy sounds were coming from the black cloud—like the screaming of a thousand demons.

Sticky warmth ran along her jaw as blood began to drip from her ears.

As she fought the wind to get to where David was standing, she could hear him reading from a section of the book in Latin at the top of his lungs. Having recognized a few of the lines, David believed it must have been the section of the book Albert had used to drive demons away. Although Albert had always said it only drove the demons out of the person, it never successfully extinguished them from existence. Right now, David would be happy if it just stopped the wind and the storm for a few moments so he could gather his thoughts. Out of the corner of his eye, he watched as Lorenza fought her way toward him. He could not stop reading—he knew that much—or all would be for naught. *Why isn't something happening? What am I doing wrong?* David thought. It seemed with every line he read, the storm increased in its strength and power. He snapped the book closed and just held it. *What use is this?* This was not some individually possessed person. This was an entire legion of demons coming to collect all life as payment for being held captive for eons in absolute nothingness.

Lorenza finally made it to his side, and he turned and looked into her eyes. Those eyes. He couldn't recall seeing eyes like hers before. So amazing and lovely. Gentle and caring, yet brilliant. He felt the impulse run through him. *I love her.* He *did* care if he died today. Reaching out, he pulled her to him and held her close to his chest.

"I love you," he said to her next to her ear and then noticed the blood. The sound and fury of the storm were taking their toll on them both. He felt his ear and looked at his fingers, finding them covered in blood.

"It's about time you realized that" she said against his chest. "I've felt that way about you since the first moment I met you. Now here, put this on!" She kissed the purple priest collar stole in the middle where the cross had been embroidered into it. Then she hung it around his neck. David looked down at it and then questioningly up into her face.

"I don't believe in God or this stuff. Never have. I refused to do this for Albert. There is no God to protect us. Just us." David started to pull it off.

"Leave it, David." Lorenza took a smaller one and did the same to it and placed it around her neck. "You may not believe in God, but he believes in you. Otherwise, you wouldn't be here today. Everything you and I have learned through a thousand lifetimes, comes down to the next few minutes. Everything." She opened the book of Holy Orders and started to read the Litany of the Saints out loud.

The wind abated around them, though beyond a three-foot radius, the storm was still raging. Roof tiles were flying off all kinds of buildings, and the air was filled with debris. David was aware a piece of stray refuse at that speed could drive a hole right through a human body. Yet, the circle around them was devoid of all wind and wreckage. It was silent and still. Two different worlds were existing in one

259

place at one time. They were in the eye of the storm, the center of the cyclone.

In the distance, they watched as a dark mass started to take shape below the black cloud. It had the proportions of a person, yet it was black, pulling in all the light around it. They were now looking upon the first being ever made by the mind of God.

"Eryther," Lorenza said quietly. "Look behind him."

Forming out of the clouds were tens of thousands of demons, each appearing out of thin air and colliding into existence over the city. The surrounding light was being swallowed by them. Each wore armor of black pounded iron and wielded weapons blindingly reflecting off the sunlight. Lorenza thought they were only the things of nightmares. But now, they were very real.

David pointed toward the East. In the sky, appeared a band of angels being led by one who David could only assume was the legendary Michael. He was on a straight course for Eryther. Both David and Lorenza saw him draw his sword. An angel's sword: the only instrument with ability to kill both demons and angels. Hundreds of angels that had stood with Lucifer perished by that blade.

Lorenza and David heard the heavenly choir—the sounds of a thousand voices that ancient prophets spoke of hearing when an angel's sword was drawn. Divine sounds preclude any battle between the righteous and the evil.

More and more demons were appearing behind their leaders. The day was growing dark around the two people on the roof, yet it was still while the sun was nearly straight above them. It was a different kind of darkness than night. It was cold and empty darkness in which no life existed.

If Michael could not hold them at bay, they would cover the city in minutes, and all the light and life would be gone. Thomas ran from the doorway, crouched to make himself small against the winds devastating Venice. He pushed toward where Lorenza and David stood. Thomas felt the training of the old boxer inside of him pushing him and giving him the power to drive his legs hard and carry him through the onslaught of wind and things within it. He could feel his skin being torn and cut by the debris hitting him. Blood was gushing from a head wound, and his legs almost failed him. When Thomas was within a foot of the circle of silence, David turned and finally saw him. David reached out and grabbed his hand and pulled Thomas into the tight ring of calm.

"Are you alright?" Lorenza knelt next to him on one knee, holding his shirt to his head to stop the bleeding.

"In comparison to what Master Bruno went through, I am the picture of health." He winced as he pulled a piece of glass from his forehead and then ripped his shirt to put a bandage on the spot. Then, with her help, he pulled himself up.

"Why are you up here?" she said while helping him to his feet. "I thought you went to find the source of the light beam."

"This." He handed her the letter, and she quickly read it.

"Oh my God, no!" She almost screamed, holding her hand to her mouth. "David, do not read anything else from that book; it is only giving them more power."

David looked at her, bewildered. "What did you say?"

"That Book is the tampered one. Whoever is using it is may be unaware they are not summoning a single demon, but they are breaking the seal on the Crystal Sphere." Lorenza looked panicked, as did Thomas and David. What could they do now to help? "The sequence of words in the book I couldn't understand and the note from Albert. He said not to read them out of order. However, two of the pages have been changed."

"Matteo!" David exclaimed.

"What?" Lorenza replied.

"On the plane, I read a note which had been tucked inside the book. Cardinal Brambilla wrote it to someone named 'Antoine.' The note described his failed endeavor to destroy the book by recounting how each time he had torn a page from it, the book attempted to guard itself against harm. He must have jumbled the order when replacing the torn pages inside."

"That's why it didn't make sense to me," Lorenza stated. "Those pages being in reversed order caused something far worse to happen."

"You mean like reading the Lord's prayer backward as some cultists do?" David asked, not sure if he was trying to be funny or now was simply hysterical.

"I guess," Lorenza said. "It has the power both ways."

Thomas pointed out toward the center of the city. The two armies were engaging. Michael was just now attacking Eryther. Their swords struck, and the entire earth shook as if there had just been a major earthquake.

The three on the roof almost lost their footing. If not demons, then the battle itself would destroy the world. Lorenza pulled her stole off her neck and handed it to Thomas, who kissed it and put it on. He picked up the book of Holy Orders and moved to the section for protection. Then, he started to read aloud.

"No!" he yelled, and the others looked at the battle scene. Angels and demons were falling from the sky. White and black as rain. Halfway toward the ground, each would explode into a puff of mist. Eryther had just run his blade into Michael's chest and tossed him off it. Michael was falling and then became nothing but smoke as well.

"Thomas continued to read." Lorenza opened the correct book to the relevant section and began to read it aloud. Instantly, a reverberation started to move across the land. As she continued to read, the wind started to decrease in speed, and they could move out from the small area they had been standing. They spread out slightly to give each other some room.

"Something is happening," David said. He was walking to the edge of the building on her far side. He noticed the waves in the Grand Canal were calming down, and the air was almost free of debris. "Keep reading, Lorenza."

"Thomas, I will run down and get some bandages for your head. Don't stop reading." David ran back to the door and dashed down the stairs to find what he needed.

Thomas looked up and watched as Eryther's head jerked toward them. Eryther had felt the power and knew what the end would be if someone finished that prayer they were saying out loud. Observing him, Thomas saw him move into flight and was now heading straight for them on the roof.

"Lorenza, do not stop reading. Please. No matter what happens." Thomas reached inside his pocket and pulled out the crucifix on the chain Father Novelli had given him, and he now understood why. He wrapped it around his right hand like a boxer wrapping his fists before a fight. He then read from the Holy Order while observing the madness unfolding before him.

Eryther was directly above them now and diving directly at Lorenza. Placing his sword before him, still covered with Michael's blood, Eryther flew toward the woman who now, was just a few feet away.

Using all the strength he had left within him, Thomas drove himself upon the tip of Eryther's sword. At the same instant, he slugged as hard as he could with his right hand into the side of the demon's face. Where the crucifix hit, the flesh was burnt away, and Eryther screamed in pain.

The sword had ripped through Thomas's midsection and Eryther was holding him up on it as he drifted from the rooftop out over the Grand Canal. Thomas's eyes still maintained life. He should have been dead but was not.

Eryther looked quizzically at the man on his sword. Why had his blow damaged him so much? Then, he looked again at the man.

His voice was deep and filled with hate as recognition overcame him. "Astaroth! How the mighty have fallen. Michael fought like a child, and now you. Pretending to be a human." Eryther turned his face with his good eye and looked closely at Thomas. The demon screamed again as he felt the poison of the crucifix running through his system. He flexed Thomas from his blade and watched as the former angel plunged toward earth.

David had made it back to the roof just as Thomas fell to his death. He felt his heart tear inside his chest. He then ran and grabbed Lorenza. "Keep reading, louder." Tears were flowing from her eyes, and short sobs were all she could get out at the sight of Thomas's death. "He knew exactly what he was doing, and so do we!"

He lifted the book back and pointed at it. Lorenza started to read again. David took one step out in front of her and pulled his own hands up in a fighting position. Wrapped around each hand was a rosary Maria had given him.

"Come on and try me, you ugly son of a bitch." David now assumed a fighter's stance.

Chapter 33

In the small, lovely garden, the cloaked figure stood next to his pond. He was watching the fish fight for some crumbs from the bread he was tossing to them. He heard something in the distance. A scream or cry that carried with it a hint of a memory.

Then, the pain struck. A pain he had not felt in a very long time. One of his own had been killed. Again, the pain came, and this time, it drove him to his knees. Lucifer sucked in air, as the pain screamed through his body. *Who could this be that is so very near?* Then, he felt it inside his being.

"Astaroth!" he whispered. "No!" He stood up, fighting the pain and ignoring it. "NO! Not you, my brother. No, no, no, no..." he screamed at the top of his lungs.

Getting back to his feet, he loosened the cord around his waist and let it drop to the ground. He pulled off his cloak and flexed once. Two great white wings extended out from his back. Twelve feet wide. Wings that hadn't been opened in an eon. Now they would be needed. He touched his breast, and golden armor encased his body. Reaching down under his bench, Lucifer pulled a great sword that slightly vibrated as he drew it from its sheath. He ran his gloved hand along the edge of his sword, observing the sharpness increase as his hand made its way from the fuller to the blade.

Very quietly, he spoke to the beautiful peacock next to him, which had turned its head upwards to carefully look at him.

"I swore once that I would never raise this sword again in anger." His fingertips still touching it ever slightly. His thoughts crying out a warning. *Please, Astaroth, do not engage. Run as a mortal should. This is no longer your battle.*

For a moment, Lucifer's mind was joined with the spirit of Astaroth, who spoke to him in his laughing and caring way. Joyous in all things, his words became pearls to Lucifer. *Let the humans fight their battle. Is this not what you always wanted? For them all to perish?* Lucifer then felt enormous pain in his solar plexus as the fatal blow was delivered to Astaroth and the living spirit fled from the body of his oldest of friends.

Lucifer knew that for Astaroth to be reborn, man had to survive. Lucifer dragged himself up and pulled into his lungs a great gulp of air and let it out slowly. "Alright." Pushing his sword into its sheath, he girded the blade's belt about his waist and picked up his golden spear. Crouching for a moment, he spoke to the peacock. "Farewell, my friend, for in the ranks of death, I find myself again." The peacock screamed its objection.

Pushing hard with his legs, Lucifer shot into the air in his dimension and streaked across the emptiness of time into another domain. A domain filled with humans.

His voice rang out loudly and filled the universe. "Asmodeus, Aza, Beelzebub, Mastema, and Kokabiel, the Star of God, bring your cohorts and legions, for again we fight!" His voice smashed through the ether.

The planet appeared to be hit by a giant electromagnetic pulse as the speakers on radios and televisions filled with static. Militaries around the globe observed thousands of striking lines like meteorites appear out of nowhere, all headed directly towards Earth.

Within seconds of his war cry, the skies over Venice filled with seasoned and furious angels, all of whom had vengeance pouring through their bloodstreams. This time, Lucifer thought, no one was going to restrain them in their assault. If it wasn't an angel or human, it would die this day.

When Lucifer appeared over Venice, a light, brighter than any sunrise, followed him like a contrail. All eyes on the ground looked up to where he hung in the sky. Lucifer, the first of the first, flew with a single-minded purpose. The scowl on his face was cruel and befitted the moment. As Lucifer pulled his sword, a single thought entered his mind – *Astaroth!*

"Attack!" Lucifer cried out, and in the moment, he did not care if his actions ended life in the entire universe, for this might indeed be his final battle. Retribution for Astaroth and all his brothers would be extracted. Today, the demons would not be sent back to imprisonment, but to the void of nothingness as though they had never existed. No demon foolish enough to engage in battle today would survive. Lucifer flung himself headlong and straight at Eryther.

Eryther had sacrificed three of his own to consume their energy to revitalize himself and heal his wound. He saw Lucifer coming and grinned. Their day had arrived, and he now flew directly at the Morning Star. Angels and demons were falling by the score from the skies over Venice, exploding into clouds of ash leaving only remnants of their existences on the cobblestone walkways and a thin film on the canals.

The angels were outnumbered five to one and with the death of Michael, many of the angels perceived the battle to be lost and hopeless. But now, watching Lucifer and their fallen brethren engaged in the battle against Eryther and his demon legion, a renewed hope returned to them. When Lucifer headed directly for Eryther all of the angels assembled behind him.

On the villa's rooftop, both David and Lorenza were held captive by the view of the battle raging just a short distance from them. There were no words to describe the scene unfolding. The scale of the battle was unbelievable, while the noise was deafening. The vision of slaughter was beyond anything imaginable. Lorenza whispered, "It's Lucifer!"

David was first to break from his trance and looked about him. He swung around to face Lorenza. "Read, Lorenza! You've got to keep reading. Start the next section; we need to drive them back and seal the breach."

Lorenza wiped the tears from her eyes, opened the book, and turned the page to the next section, which represented the hammer to close the break and seal it again. She began reading aloud. "Daemon vetus timeant te. Fear thee, old demon." The start of the invocation of sealing the Crystal Sphere. The most dreaded words a demon could hear, intoned by a human.

Sensing the book's energy, Eryther twisted in flight and redirected his attention on Lorenza. She was holding the one thing in the universe he truly feared.

Chapter 34

As Lorenza continued reading from the book, David saw the change over the battlefield first. The funnel cloud was starting to pull demons back into it. *We are beginning to seal the breach!* David thought. His eyes then noticed movement coming directly toward them. *Eryther!* David's mind whirled in alarm. *He must sense what we are doing!*

"We are forcing them back inside!" David said. "Keep reading! It's working!"

Lorenza looked up and saw Eryther coming directly at her. She raised to her full height and started to read even louder. David again stepped in front of her, his fist covered with rosaries. All the fear had drained out of him. All that was left was his love for Lorenza and his desire to kill this 'creature' coming at her. David had never experienced such coldness in his soul. His mind was clear; he only regretted he had not told Lorenza the truth earlier than he did. Outside of that, he was ready to meet the next mystery and see where it would lead him. If he could not stop this demon, then Lorenza would die as well. That thought hit him, and the adrenaline pumped through his system like pistons in an engine. His eyes went wild with red rage; he bared his teeth and pulled back his right hand.

Eryther laughed seeing another mortal setting to strike him. The last time he had fought all of God's angels, he had almost won; this now was an apathetic display. He would bring darkness to half of the universe and devour billions of souls. He looked carefully at the woman knowing she was the real threat, for she held the weapon. He needed to destroy the book.

Just as Eryther approached the villa to strike down Lorenza, the flat side of a sword hit him directly in his back. He plummeted to the cobbles below. Attempting to right himself, a foot slammed into his chest, and another pinned down his sword arm. Lucifer glared down at him, tilting his head sideways to look deeply at the abomination known as Eryther. Lucifer realized he had never seen him up close and wanted to study him for a moment before he consigned him to nothingness and oblivion.

David turned to Lorenza. "You have got to read fast, Lorenza; otherwise, you know better than anyone, Lucifer and the angels will kill them all. If that happens, we are all finished."

Lorenza nodded to him, placed her finger on the text, and started to read the sentences much quicker than before, not concerning herself over slight mispronunciations. She had two pages to go, and then hopefully, this would be done—two pages each with thirty-four lines, eight words per line. *Read faster*, she told herself. Her body started to rock backward and forward like she had seen so many Hassidic Jews do while praying. *Five hundred and forty-four words*, she calculated. *Each taking just less than a second to recite*. She still had a good five or six minutes of speaking. Lorenza couldn't bear to look up and see what advancement Lucifer's cohort was having on the demons. Time. She needed more time.

***

Inside the Scuola Grande di San Rocca, Cardinal Zimmerman was confused and frightened. Standing in the middle of the marble floor, he was being hunted by two shedim that had found him. All the preparation, the work, the learning, and the one thing he desired most, the proof of their existence, was now the one thing that was going to kill him. *I can't control them!* A dark mist began filling the candle-lit room and the smell of burnt leather filled his nostrils.

What have I done?

The light from the candles slowly dimmed as a hand grasped his throat. He tried to fight back but could not. He let out a gurgle of fear before the darkness overtook him. The book the old man had been holding vanished along with him, leaving only the beaded rosary lying on the floor.

Chapter 35

Lorenza could not read any faster for fear of missing a single word. All the stories she had heard about the physical pain scribes went through to copy a scared manuscript. One letter at a time, taking as much as an hour to write one sentence. The demand for holding one breath in between words and then breathing as deeply as she could. It all came back. So much like the Jewish Shema Yisrael, the holiest of holies. The tenant of all faiths in the Western World. The first verse encapsulates the monotheistic essence of Judaism; therefore, all faiths were built upon it. She rocked back and forth in a trance with a rhythm, allowing herself to feel the words while sending her soul out with them.

For what I am to the universe? her mind asked. If she died here and yet sealed the breach, her life would be complete and for a great purpose. *What more could anyone ever ask?* She raised her head and spoke so God could see her. So, God could hear her. Uncovered and unafraid. "For I am me, and that means I am all of us." She flipped the page.

"I had forgotten just how much I hate you." Eryther spat the words out as Lucifer pushed down harder with his foot on the demon's chest.

"I have never forgotten you. I hated the day my Lord demanded I not kill you outright for what you might bring to the universe," Lucifer said with contempt in his voice. "I no longer care. To see you die is worth my essence, life, and anything else I have ever possessed. You killed my brother. You killed Astaroth! And for that sin, you will die this day at my hands." Lucifer raised his spear high over his shoulder, pointing to the center of Eryther's chest and his black heart.

On the rooftop, Lorenza looked up to heaven and spoke the final words—the same Jesus had used on the cross. *"Mem Shin Lamed Mem! – It is Finished."* She closed the book and waited.

A powerful wind began raging. From all directions, it engulfed all those who had come into the universe uninvited. Over the battlefield in the sky, the demons were being whirled upward into the

278

funnel cloud, leaving only angels left floating in an open sky.

On the street below, Eryther was dragged up off the cobbles and twisted in the air without the ability to control himself, before becoming a formless mass that was pulled at tremendous speed into the eye of the cloud, which drew into itself and closed.

Lucifer threw down his spear onto the cobbles and leaned back with arms outstretched, fist clenched, and screamed in anguish toward Heaven, "NOOO!"

On the rooftop, David walked over and put his arm around Lorenza's shoulder, pulling her close. He wanted to say something but thought better of it. For now, he just wanted to hold her. *We did it*, he thought, as both of his arms now embraced Lorenza. *Holy crap, we did it!*

Epilogue

A solitary figure walked through the rain pouring down on St. Mark's Square. He thought about the blood of martyrs, holy men and women of different beliefs, all wrongly convicted of crimes that never existed to which this square had stood witness. He thought of his friend, Astaroth, who made the choice long ago to live as a man. His friend who opted to become an active participant in the human experience with all its attendant treasures and misfortunes: love and hate, fear and comfort, birth...and death.

As the tears fell from his eyes, the winds began to still, and where once there were clouds, beams of sunlight hit his face. The clouds began to separate and opened to move in around him. From above, he heard the voice he had not heard in an eon. *Lucifer, my Morning Star, there is something I need to tell you...*

AN APOLOGY TO LUCIFER

About the Authors

Wayne Haley is a retired University Administrator who has been writing for pleasure for thirty-five years. Wayne spends most of his free time with his wife, Kathleen, walking the beaches near his home in Hawaii.

Sean Haley has spent the past twenty-five years serving as the Chief Compliance Officer for several investment firms. Now living outside of Los Angeles, Sean spends much of his free time with his wonderful wife, Kristy, and their blended family of five children - usually shuttling them to various activities and sporting events. Wayne and Sean are currently working on their next collaborative work.

OTHER EXQUISITE FICTION FROM
D. X. VAROS

CPSIA information can be obtained
at www.ICGtesting.com
Printed in the USA
BVHW080936310522
638501BV00008B/176